The Scythe's Secrets

A Tessa Randolph Cozy Mystery, Volume 2

Christine Zane Thomas and Paula Lester

Published by Paula Lester and Christine Zane Thomas, 2020.

Chapter 1

"But I'm scared of heights." Tessa scowled to hide the horrified expression trying to jump onto her face. "You're my mother. You should know that. I can't even ride the Ferris wheel without getting dizzy."

"I thought you grew out of that," Cheryl said.

"No. I grew out of going to amusement parks. Can't you give this assignment to someone else?"

"Don't be ridiculous. It's part of your job. I can't keep track of what the agents like and don't like. We can't cherry-pick our jobs." Cheryl glanced up from the computer and the corners of her mouth twitched upward. She had gained immunity to her daughter's unhappy expressions decades earlier. In fact, the grumpier Tessa got and the deeper she scowled, the more amused Cheryl became. "Mr. Hanson is scheduled to die of natural causes today, and you're his reaper. He dies. You escort his soul to the afterlife. That's that."

Tessa flopped into the chair across from Cheryl with a huff and wondered about her career choice. It was bad enough to have a mother who erred quite forcefully on the critical side of the fence. But having her also be your boss was a flavor of crazy most people would know to avoid. "Why can't I just reap him when he gets to the ground?"

Cheryl rolled her eyes. "He isn't going to die on the ground. He's going to die about halfway down." She considered. "Or up, depending on how you look at it."

"I'd rather be looking up."

Cheryl tapped at her keyboard and read something on the screen. "Yes. His heart will give out. Which isn't terribly surprising—it *is* his ninetieth birthday."

"Today?" Tessa squeaked. "He's going to die on his birthday?"

"It's not as uncommon as you'd think. And what a way to go—his file says he started skydiving every year on his birthday when he turned sixty." She waved a hand. "But he goes a lot more than that, of course. He's a certified instructor. So, just show up for the time slot I booked for you to dive with him." Cheryl got to her feet. "There's really no choice here. You have to be there when it happens, which is going to be while he's in the air."

"But—"

"No buts! What if the poor man's soul gets trapped in his body as it floats to the ground? That would be awful."

"But—"

"Theresa. What if he gets stuck midair? His spirit could leave the body and take off in the wind while you're standing there twiddling your thumbs. You don't want to lose another soul, do you?"

Tessa bit back a curse and shook her head grudgingly. "No. Once is enough."

Cheryl touched her perfect inverted bob in several spots as though to be sure no strands had suddenly wrestled free from their bonds of mega-super-strength hair spray. "Don't worry. There's no order in the system for a reaper for *you*. Apparently, your parachute will bring you safely to the ground."

"You're enjoying this too much."

"You may like skydiving." Cheryl's lips twitched with barely contained mirth. "Ooh, maybe you'll start going once a year on *your* birthday too. You could completely lose your fear of heights today, Theresa. Wouldn't that be nice?"

"It would be *nice* if you remembered I like to be called Tessa. And you're right. Maybe I'll love skydiving. I hope I do. They'll be looking for a new instructor at this skydiving place after today, right? I'm going to think of this as a job interview. There's no way the boss could be worse than the one I already have."

Cheryl didn't appear worried. She waved a hand and herded Tessa out of the office. "Have fun, dear. Don't be late to the death."

"I wouldn't dream of it." Tessa rolled her eyes as she headed out of the office and into the bright sunlight of the parking lot.

Briefly, she glanced over her shoulder at the run-down building—her current workplace. It was disguised as a dilapidated life insurance office in an attempt to keep most humans away from what was really a grim reaper agency.

In the few months since Tessa had started her new job, she'd gotten used to the routine. Get up, check for assignments on the reaper app on her phone, reap souls. The app gave Tessa a good chuckle every time she saw the icon. It, too, had a disguise, designed to look like a cycle tracker to keep any random person who picked up the phone from clicking on it.

If there were no assignments on the app, Tessa headed into the office and did paperwork or sat in Gloria's office and chatted with her fellow reaper until Cheryl gave them both a death glare. It was an expression her mother had perfected having worked so many years as a grim reaper herself.

But it had turned out to be a pretty decent job overall. The pay was good. Tessa hadn't had to worry about making rent since her first assignment. And she'd even been able to pay for her landlord, Silas, to make some much needed upgrades to Linda.

Tessa ran her hand over the car's red hood. "How you doing, girl? Any aches or pains?"

Linda didn't answer but she started right up when Tessa turned the key. Progress. Since Silas had started taking care of her, the car did that much more often than before.

The drive out to Mist River Skydiving School was about twenty minutes, which was more than enough time to get worked up about the idea of jumping out of a plane.

Worked up into a panic. It wasn't like she was completely risk averse. She'd recently taken up mountain biking after coming across an almost new bike for a good price at a yard sale. And Tessa often dreamed about a SCUBA certificate. After all, she planned to retire to some tropical island far away from Michigan's cold winters. Maybe she could get a head start on those plans later this week while attending the reaper convention in Florida.

But skydiving? That was never on her list. It, along with wearing thong bikinis and eating anything made with ghost peppers, was something Tessa thought she'd never do. But it was just like this job to prove her wrong. She could only hope that reaping and thongs would stay far apart.

As Tessa pulled into the flight school's dusty parking lot, she regretted the greasy bacon and eggs she'd had for breakfast, which rolled around like her stomach was an old-style butter churn.

She pulled a cross-body purse over her head, closed the car door, and forced reluctant feet to move toward the school. It was a huge, bright red, steel-sided building divided in half, one part an open hanger bay containing a small plane and the other an office space. When she entered the office side, a box above the door played a cheerful, tinny little tune.

Tessa scanned the lobby, which sported hard plastic chairs and framed pictures of smiling people wearing flight suits and looking relieved to be alive.

She thought of Mr. Hanson and how this would be his last jump. A tiny lump formed in her throat, but she swallowed it away. He was ninety and would go doing something he loved.

Plus, he'd have his own personal reaper right there, ready to show him the way to the other side, where, presumably, the next phase of his soul's journey awaited.

"Morning, you! You're right on time."

Tessa spun at the sound of the male voice and found a nice-looking thirty-something guy with dark hair smiling at her. She drew her hand up and waved with her fingers shyly. "Hi."

The man stuck out his hand. "Bryce Hanson."

"I'm, um, Tessa Randolph."

He squeezed it gently and smiled bigger. "Welcome, Um Tessa Randolph."

"Just Tessa."

"Okay, Just Tessa."

Tessa chuckled, then her forehead scrunched. "Mr. Hanson? Are you . . . my instructor?" If this guy was celebrating his ninetieth birthday, Tessa wanted to know his secret for maintaining youth before she let him go into the great beyond.

Bryce chuckled. "My grandpa and I are, yeah."

Ah. "So, this is a family business?"

"It is now." Bryce nodded. "Grandpa came here for the first time when he turned sixty. It was love at first jump, and he eventually became an instructor and helped me learn. I bought the place five years ago, with Grandpa co-signing." He crossed his arms and leaned back on his heels, chest puffing. "It's been a great run."

"Wow. Well, congratulations. It's great to do something you love."

He nodded and then gestured toward a second room. "Let's get started. You're our only jumper today. There's a couple videos to watch and a few other bits of training to do, and then you can get your AFF on."

"My what?"

"Accelerated Free Fall. It's the type of skydiving we do here."

Tessa swallowed hard. "Accelerated? Does that mean it's faster than regular skydiving?" She forced herself to follow Bryce out of the lobby and into a small conference room.

"Not faster. You ever heard of terminal velocity?"

"I've heard of it," she said. "But I've never felt it."

"Nervous?" Bryce fiddled with a computer, and a projection screen on the wall lit up.

"A little," she admitted.

"Well, don't be. Grandpa and I know what we're doing. And AFF is the best way to experience the exhilaration of a real free fall." He winked. "It's gonna be fun."

"Sure, it is." She wasn't convinced. She may not die during the flight, but she could absolutely squeal like a ninny and embarrass herself. Not that the elder Mr. Hanson would be able to tell anyone.

But the video was interesting, and by the time it was over, Tessa felt a little more at ease.

Bryce led her into the hanger where a man who looked like an older version of him, only with white hair, stood eating a sandwich. "This is my grandfather, Bryce Hanson."

"But—"

"I know." Bryce nodded. "I'm a third. I used to go by Trey. But these days, I'm Bryce and this is Instructor Hanson."

The elderly man wiped a hand on his pants and shook Tessa's. "It's a great day for a first-time jumper," he said. His voice was gravely, like you'd expect of a nonagenarian but otherwise, he looked hale and healthy. Hard to believe his ticker was on its last few beats.

He gestured to a platter with more food. "Hungry for lunch?"

"I'll pass." Tessa didn't relish the thought of having a full stomach when she did her jump. "Happy birthday, by the way."

His bushy eyebrows rose. "How'd you know it's my birthday?"

Oops. "Your grandson told me."

The younger Bryce had crossed the room to talk to a woman wearing a neat uniform with black epaulettes on her shoulders, who Tessa figured was their pilot, so he didn't hear the lie.

"Ah. Well, thank you. But, at my age, every day's a happy day to be alive. Has to be. You never know when you'll be done with this world." He popped the last bite of sandwich into his mouth and gestured for Tessa to follow him to a wall lined with hanging flight suits and other equipment. "Let's get you fitted."

The next hour passed quickly as Bryce and the elder Instructor Hanson helped Tessa get fitted and showed her how to use the parachute, even taking her outside onto a big grassy lawn to practice.

The two men had an easy relationship. It was obvious they were fond of each other. When Bryce ran inside to get something, she said as much to his grandfather. "I wish my mom and I got along like the two of you do," she added.

The older man studied her for a moment, pursing his lips. Then he smiled, revealing a cracked tooth in front. "Ya know, that's the thing about life. It's easy to spend a lot of time thinking about how imperfect things are. How you'd like it to be different. A person can literally while away years doin' that. If you want something to change, Miss Randolph, you have to force it to. Be the daughter you want to be and let the rest fall into place."

The moment felt profound—like Instructor Hanson was imparting his last words of wisdom onto Tessa. Like he was instructing her in more than skydiving. She felt a little guilty—it should've been the man's grandson who got to hear that, not her.

Bryce jogged over to them. "All set?"

"Yes, sir! Let's get in the air." Tessa took the older man's elbow as he led toward the hangar. "Fifteen minutes from now, you'll be on the ground again. I always have a beer to celebrate a good landing. Maybe you and my grandson will join me." He winked.

"Maybe." She gave him a bright smile and let him lead her to the plane.

The Hansons helped keep Tessa upright and oriented during the free fall part of the jump. She was shocked to find it exhilarating, fun, and only slightly terrifying.

Bryce peeled away first, signaling it was time to release her chute. Tessa held onto Instructor Hanson a moment longer. She held his gaze, waiting for the moment his heart would stop. And when it did, Tessa reached out with her other hand, signaling for the portal to the other side.

His face relaxed and his mouth turned upward as a bright white light spread out below their feet.

It felt like time stopped for a moment as she watched him move forward into the light, pausing to give her a jaunty wave. Then, the light was gone, and she was falling fast. Quickly, she reached to pull her chute. She held her breath, and it opened.

Mr. Hanson's automatic reserve chute opened a few seconds later, and his body floated gently down a distance beside her.

Tessa drew in a breath and braced for dual impact of the hard ground and Bryce's inevitable heartbreak.

Chapter 2

Tessa stayed with Bryce until the ambulance had come and gone with his grandfather's body and some other Hanson family members showed up. That wasn't part of her job description, but it was the right thing to do.

Once she was satisfied the young man was supported by his parents and cousins, Tessa slipped away. She drove Linda to the Mist River Manor apartments with a heavy heart, reminding herself that the elder Bryce Hanson was ninety years old and seemed happy to go over to the unknown.

That was what got Tessa through the grim business of reaping. When it came time, most of her clients were ready. Then there was Chet Sanborn, the soul who'd given her so much trouble, eluding her for days until Tessa caught his killer—almost meeting her own end in the process.

She shuddered at the thought. Hopefully, nothing like that ever happened again.

The apartment lobby was deserted. Tessa checked her mailbox and immediately rolled her eyes, tossing the flyer for a local cable company into a nearby recycling bin. She split WiFi with a friend in the building and used a streaming service. Didn't everybody? *Cable is dead.* Only, it didn't seem to realize yet that yet.

When she turned to head for her apartment, the lobby wasn't empty anymore. Silas St. Onge, the building's superintendent and maintenance guy extraordinaire—also the mechanical magician who kept Linda purring—stood gaping like a caught fish. As usual, a chunk of sandy blond hair flopped over one of his eyes.

Usually, Silas was pretty cool and collected. But now, he appeared to be struggling. Shocked about something, maybe? Tessa couldn't help herself. Curiousness overcame her, and she walked up to him, tipping her head. "Everything okay?"

He blinked a few times as though having trouble focusing on her and then, suddenly, a wide smile broke across his face. To Tessa's delight, it was big enough to reveal the adorable dimple in his right cheek.

"I can't believe it." He held out his arm. "Can you pinch me? Make sure I'm not dreaming."

Her gaze dropped to his muscular arm and the bicep that strained the short sleeve. She pursed her lips and gave it a light pinch then shrugged. "You seem real enough to me. I think you're awake. I'm awake. And I have been since way too early this morning."

"You think eight am is way too early," he said.

"Because it is," Tessa countered. "So, what's up? Why do you think you're dreaming?"

He shook his head and dropped the arm again. "Mrs. Cross just gave me five thousand dollars." His tone was hushed, matching the awed expression on his face perfectly. "She just *gave* it to me. No strings attached."

"Wow! That's nice of her." Tessa couldn't help but gasp. She totally understood Silas's conundrum. That was a shock.

Mrs. Cross lived a few doors down from Tessa. She was an elderly woman who always had her nose just a bit too far into the other residents' business, but she was sweet and mostly harmless. *But sweet enough to give someone five thousand dollars?*

"Yeah, she gave me half of what she won because I get her groceries for her. I picked out the winning scratch-off ticket. She said it was only fair. I tried to turn it down, but she insisted." He ran a hand through his hair pushing back the floppy piece. "I have no idea what to do with it. Bank it for a rainy day, I guess."

Tessa leaned an elbow on the lobby's front counter. "That's so boring."

"You know me." He shrugged and put his hands in his pocket.

He was right. She did know him. They'd become close over the past few months, ever since Tessa's breakup with Frank and since starting her new job as a grim reaper. But Silas couldn't know about that.

She considered for a minute, thinking about Silas and his hardworking attitude. He worked on his days off. He maintained Linda for next to nothing but a pat on the back. Tessa had always been a hard worker, but she'd never had Silas's work ethic. She liked to put her feet up whenever possible. What would she do if a big sum of money fell into her lap? "I know! You should take a vacation."

He grimaced like vacations were torture. "Why would I do that?"

Yep. She knew Silas, all right. She snorted. "To relax like a normal person for more than a minute and a half? I mean, I'm starting to think you're a workaholic. If you aren't fixing something around here are getting groceries for elderly residents, you're working on Linda for just the cost of parts."

Silas wasn't convinced but his wince dissolved into a thoughtful expression.

"You deserve a break more than anybody I know," she pressed.

He shrugged. "Lots of people work harder than I do."

A sudden thought leaped into Tessa's mind and before she'd slowed down to examine it, she blurted out, "You know I'm going to Florida in a couple days. It's a work conference at the Salt Water Resort in Miami Beach. I don't think all of the rooms are taken."

That was weird, right? Why had she said that? Now her landlord was going to think she was imagining him in swim trunks lounging by the pool. Which she totally was, but it was super embarrassing to be caught thinking it.

Silas cocked his head with a come again type expression.

"I mean, you could go anywhere, really. I just mention it in case you want to have somebody you know around. You know, on your vacation. Someone there to have dinner or drinks or something with." Tessa stammered to a halt and pressed her lips together to stem the tide of awkward rambling.

"You know, that does sound like fun. But I'm not sure what I'd do about this place." He waved a hand vaguely at the ceiling, then sighed, considering.

"What?" Tessa questioned the sigh.

Silas shook his head. "It's just my buddy Jason owes me a favor. A few favors. He could probably fill in for a few days or something. I'll have to think about it."

Pushing herself away from the desk, Tessa nodded. "Good. Well, do that. And congratulations on the windfall. I'd better run." She headed toward the door leading to her apartment's hallway.

"Bye." Silas seemed distracted.

Maybe he was imagining Tessa in her swimsuit next to the pool in Florida? She groaned and clamped down on the thought. Silas was nice but he'd never really flirted with Tessa. Why would he be thinking that?

He wasn't. He was probably thinking about the disarray the apartment would go in if he did leave. Or, maybe, he was considering the sun and relaxation—the thought of a cocktail or two. Yeah, that was it, for sure.

Feeling a little better, Tessa let herself into the tiny apartment she kept clean and tidy, mostly because she didn't have too much stuff. Her new job was rapidly helping her get square on past-due bills and things but there wasn't much left over to indulge in her desire to buy a dozen brand-name purses yet.

Her small tortie, Pepper, rubbed on Tessa's leg, purring louder than such a tiny little thing should be able to.

"Hey, cutie. It's good to see you too. Are you hungry?"

The cat sat on her haunches and yowled mournfully.

"Oh, I see. You're actually about to starve to death, huh?"

Pepper inclined her chin in a motion that made her look haughty and meowed more softly.

"I did so feed you breakfast this morning. Don't lie." Tessa crossed to the kitchen and poured some kibble into the cat's bowl. "There you go."

Pepper didn't move. She narrowed her eyes and coughed.

Tessa mimicked the cat's expression. "Don't you threaten me with a hairball, missy. You don't need canned food right now. Eat the kibble—it's good for your teeth."

Pepper raised her nose and stalked away, down the short hall to Tessa's bedroom.

"You behave!" Tessa hurried after the cat and found her curled at the foot of the bed. "Good girl."

Later, Tessa pulled a rolling suitcase out of the closet, and the tortie lifted her head. "Yes, I'm going on a trip. You'll be fine. Abi is going to feed you and clean your box while I'm gone."

A rumbling purr erupted from the feline's throat.

"You like Abi, remember? Plus, it'll give you plenty of alone time. I know how much I annoy you." Tessa grinned and shook her head. She patted Pepper's rump and set to work gathering the clothes she'd need for a few days at the conference.

And as she packed her swimsuit, she hardly thought about Silas with his shirt off at all.

Chapter 3

There was an unfamiliar car in the lot at work the next morning. Tessa wondered if someone was in there trying to buy life insurance. It wouldn't be the first time, but it was a rare occurrence. There was a protocol—forms and brochures. Real ones that paid real money upon death. All part of the guise.

But in the lobby, a man and woman stood talking to Cheryl.

Nope. Not random laypeople.

It was clear the two strangers in the lobby were related to the reaper business. For one, they were talking to Cheryl, who would never come out of her office to intercept a wayward insurance buyer. For two, the woman gave off a certain air. It couldn't really be called an aura. It was more like a vibe. Whatever it was, Tessa had learned to identify other reapers by it since she'd gotten her own powers.

The woman looked to be around Cheryl's age—late fifties or early sixties. She wore a light gray pantsuit that almost exactly matched the color of her straight, bluntly cut, shoulder-length hair.

"Ah, there she is. Our new reaper." Cheryl gestured for Tessa to join them. "My daughter, Theresa Randolph. This is April Henderson."

"Tessa," she corrected, giving April's hand a firm shake.

"Pleasure," April said. "It's always nice to keep things in the family. I just never had time to start one of those."

"April's the district supervisor for the eastern United States and Canada," Cheryl added.

"Oh." Tessa was caught off-guard. She knew her mother had bosses, but she never expected to meet them. At least, not here in the shabby office. At the convention, there were sure to be loads of other reapers.

And speaking of, Tessa's eyes flitted to the man next to and slightly behind the supervisor. Only, now that they were in closer proximity, she noted that he didn't exude the same vibe, not that of another reaper. Still, she waited for an introduction to him too.

April's gaze followed Tessa's, and she appeared a little surprised to find the twenty-something man standing there. Whether she just didn't understand social cues or was intentionally rude wasn't clear, but the woman didn't bother to introduce him. She gave Tessa a curt smile, then turned to address Cheryl. "I have something important to discuss with you. Let's use your office." She cast a cool gaze at her male companion. "You, stay put."

Tessa felt her eyebrows climb at the rudeness.

After the office door clicked shut behind the two women, Tessa smiled at the abandoned man.

He gave her an awkward little wave. "I'm Timothy. April's assistant."

"Hi, Timothy. Nice to meet you."

He was tall and lanky, with nondescript features and an ill-fitting blue suit. He wore glasses. And for some reason, Tessa couldn't help but think of an accountant when she looked at him.

She crossed the room to examine the Danishes on display on the small coffee cart there. It was not a typical day in the office. Cheryl must've brought these in for the guests. And she could tell they were from her favorite shop, just down the road from her childhood home—the house Cheryl still occupied alone.

Score!

"What brings you two to Mist River?" Tessa asked as Timothy trailed along behind her.

"Oh, you know, it's just routine mainly. April likes to visit each of her branch offices once a quarter. She has a standing competition with the western district supervisor, Lee, about who can get to all their branches most often."

He grabbed a cinnamon roll and took a big bite. A dollop of cream cheese frosting dove onto his jacket lapel like a fighter jet doing a dive maneuver. It crashed into a horrible blob. Timothy frowned and dabbed at the sticky mess with a napkin, making it much worse. "I don't think we'll be here for long."

"No?"

Giving up on the spot, he tossed the napkin in a trash can and then leaned close to Tessa. "Lee's visited one more office than April, and she wants to catch up before they see each other at the conference."

Tessa chose a simple glazed donut. Her favorite. And a lot less likely to end up with a mess on her outfit. Then she poured herself a cup of coffee.

Raised voices floated through Cheryl's door. Tessa jerked her chin that direction. "Getting the most visits in is one thing. But do you know what's going on in there?"

Timothy, having finished off the cinnamon roll, got himself a cup of coffee too. "I do. But I shouldn't say anything."

And for a moment, it seemed as if he was going to stick to that. He eyed Tessa warily, then he glanced toward the office door and lowered his voice. "Okay. But you didn't hear it from me. There's a discrepancy in the numbers. Not enough souls have been taken this month, despite the number of allotments sent to each agency." He squared his shoulders, thin chest puffing like a rooster. "It's my job to keep the books for the whole eastern district."

Tessa tried to look appropriately concerned but her mind raced. Did this have something to do with her? She'd had an . . . eventful first week on the job. But, no, the number of souls she'd reaped had been right on. The spirits' identities were what had been off a bit.

Timothy must have noticed her uneasy expression because he waved a hand. "Oh, there's nothing to worry about. We think we've pinpointed the agency involved, and it's *not* Mist River. It's the place we're headed to next. The last stop before the conference."

Tessa opened her mouth to ask him which office that was but shut it again when Cheryl's office door opened. April emerged, heading straight for the front door. "Come on, Timothy," she ordered without even sparing a glance for her assistant.

With an apologetic smile, a quick look down at the stain on his lapel, and another awkward wave, Timothy followed his boss outside.

Cheryl stood, arms crossed, gazing out at the parking lot. Tessa went to stand beside her mother. She finished her donut.

"So, your boss is . . . interesting," Tessa ventured.

A grunt was the only response, along with a deepening frown.

"Did she give you a hard time or something?"

Finally, Cheryl stirred, leveling a calm stare at Tessa. "Are you packed for the conference?"

It took a minute for Tessa to switch gears. Obviously, her mother didn't want to talk about the interaction with April.

"Uh," Tessa focused on the question about her readiness for travel. "Yeah, I guess. I mean, a few days at a resort in Florida doesn't take much in the way of clothes. I packed a couple swimsuits and a few business casual outfits." She shrugged. "I should be good to go."

"Didn't you read the last email?" Cheryl asked.

"I, uh, I think so."

"Well, are you dressing up for the theme days? I believe I have a Hawaiian shirt you can borrow. For the costume day, make sure it's an appropriate length. And don't try to be cute. There's always one person who thinks it's funny to go as a grim reaper."

"Noted," Tessa said. She had planned to skip the optional theme days.

"One last thing." Cheryl's eyes darted toward the parking lot. April and Timothy were gone. "Don't forget this is a work trip, not a vacation. Keep your wits about you." She made eye contact again. "Pay attention. You might learn something."

"Yeah, yeah. I'll be sure to take notes and come back with extra reaper tricks up my robes." Tessa laughed. "Get it? Up my robes? Like . . . reaper robes?"

"What did I just say about the costume day?" Cheryl rolled her eyes, went into her office, and shut the door without another word.

Tessa grinned, feeling like she'd won that round of good-natured sparring. But she couldn't help but think her mom might have it even worse than she did in the mean old boss category. April seemed like a real treat.

Tessa pushed aside the thought and headed to her cramped office, already dreaming of sitting by the pool with her friend Gloria in Florida, skipping as many presentations as possible to sip daiquiris and soak up the sun.

Not a vacation, my backside.

Chapter 4

"I hate layovers. Don't you?" Tessa slumped into the uncomfortable airport chair. "So boring. I wish the agency would have sprung for a direct flight." Cheryl had claimed it was agency policy to find the cheapest flights. But what kind of supernatural agency pinches pennies, really? Tessa was sure the policy was her mother's and her mother's alone.

She checked her watch. "I mean, it would've been nice to explore Chicago or something but there's not enough time. This layover is just long enough to be annoying but not long enough to be any fun."

Gloria's perfect mauve-covered lips twitched upward. "I know it's not technically a vacation. But I don't care if there's a layover—I'm just glad to be out of the office." Her grin got wider. "I'm content sitting here thinking about how Cheryl's probably going to have to fill in on a job or two while we're gone. There's bound to be enough business that Jake and Cathy can't handle it alone. How long do you think it's been since your mom reaped someone?"

Tessa shook her head. It was something she hadn't given much thought to. This used to be her mother's full-time job. She shuddered at the thought of her mother escorting someone to the other side. Or would ushering be a better word? Cheryl was so uptight and schedule-oriented—she'd probably clap her hands and say, "Chop-chop!"

"I don't know," she said. "But I guess you're right. Any time out of this office is like a vacation, huh?"

"How about we spice it up?" Gloria stood, grabbed her suitcase's handle, and started walking across the terminal.

"Okay..." Tessa hurried to grab her own luggage—they'd both just brought carry-on-sized bags to avoid the possibility of a lost suitcase putting a serious damper on their trip—and power-walked after her co-worker. "Where are we going?'

Over her shoulder, Gloria said, "The bar, of course. There are Tiki drinks with our names on them."

Tessa had never been big on drinking on airplanes. She liked to be clear-headed in case something went wrong and she needed to think fast. But she had to admit that having a drink during the layover sounded like more fun than passing the time in a hard, plastic chair staring at the runway.

Gloria paused in the doorway of an Irish pub and waited for Tessa to catch up. "I guess the Tiki will have to wait for Miami. It looks like everybody's in here."

"Everybody?"

"The other reapers from Chicago on north. Look." She nodded toward the dimly lit bar.

Following her friend's gaze, Tessa realized Gloria was right. Many of the folks sitting at the bar or gathered at round tables gave off reaper vibes.

Gloria made her way to a tall table near a window overlooking the concourse, where people bustled along in both directions, hurrying to make connecting flights. Tessa climbed into the chair and checked the laminated card advertising drink specials. When a waiter wearing a pilot's hat with a shamrock affixed to the front came by, both reapers ordered cosmos.

Gloria leaned over the tiny table. "See that guy? That's Art. He's out of Minneapolis. Has a reputation for giving each of his clients' last trips a bit of an artistic flare."

"What does *that* mean?" Tessa studied the man Gloria had indicated. He stood at the bar holding a glass of Guinness and telling a story to several other reapers, who listened with rapt attention before bursting out into guffaws. Art had hawkish features, but they didn't give him a predatory air. Instead, Tessa felt drawn to him.

Gloria laid her hands flat on the table. "Okay, so here's an example. There was a guy Art was scheduled to reap who liked burlesque shows. So, Art dressed up as the guy's favorite character—I don't know who—I just know it involved a bright orange cape and a rhinestone-studded mask. Anyway, Ari wore the outfit when he showed up to cross the guy over. He was so over-the-moon he barely noticed he was dying." Gloria chuckled.

And she laughed even louder at the look on Tessa's face as she pictured Art in drag.

"Art likes to make a production of things. Oh, and that's Shirley. I'm surprised she hasn't retired yet. She's been reaping since my grandmother was in grade school. She's from British Columbia."

The woman Gloria motioned toward was playing darts in the back corner with another reaper. Her black and silver hair was arranged in one heavy braid that reached her waist. She clapped as her dart made it into the bullseye. Then she celebrated with a chug of something in a martini glass.

Gloria's eyes scanned the crowd as the waiter dropped off their drinks. "And that's Bubba—he's from Seattle. He's a hoot at parties. I bet he'll be the guy dancing on the pool deck at the hotel."

Tessa wondered how she'd remember all these reapers' names. Still, it was fun to hear the stories. Gloria seemed to know everyone.

"That's Lydia and Cynthia. They always meet up at conferences and room together. Lydia's from Detroit and Cynthia's out of Chicago." Gloria frowned a little, setting down her pink drink. "Hmm . . . Cynthia doesn't look that good, does she?"

Tessa tried to check out the woman Gloria indicated without being obvious about it. Cynthia was slumped forward, elbows arranged on the table so her arms formed a protective circle around a margarita. Lydia had a hand on Cynthia's arm and wore a sympathetic expression as she played with the straw in her own drink. Cynthia wiped at her eyes like she was tired.

"Chicago, huh? You know, there was a guy in our office back home yesterday. Timothy—he's the assistant to the district supervisor."

"April?" Gloria's eyes went wide. "I'm glad I missed running into her."

Tessa nodded. "She was pretty icy. But anyway, Timothy told me there was some problem at the Chicago reaper office. The numbers of souls reaped versus the orders put in aren't adding up or something like that."

"Huh. I wonder what's going on. I'll have to corner Cynthia at the hotel and get the scoop."

"Do you think maybe it's Cynthia's fault?"

"No. Probably just some kind of accounting error. April likes to create waves where there should be smooth sailing. It's her leadership style." Gloria held up her glass to clink with Tessa's. "Anyway, we'd better drink up. The plane will be boarding in ten minutes."

Twenty minutes later, having consumed their cosmos way too fast, they were settling into their seats on the plane, having stowed their carry-ons in the overhead compartment. Gloria had asked for the aisle seat. "I feel too claustrophobic by the window."

"Fine with me." Tessa loved watching takeoff and landing out the window.

"It's time to move this party to the beach," Gloria said excitedly. "There will be even more reapers at the hotel bar. Plus, the hotel has a couple of nice restaurants. I'll be ready for a nice juicy steak after we get settled in the room."

Tessa was glad she was getting a chance to go to the conference and spend time with Gloria. The other reaper was fashionable and fun, and Tessa had really been enjoying getting to know her.

She opened her mouth to suggest they find some good Mexican instead. Cynthia's margarita had looked good. But raised voices drew their attention toward the front of the plane.

Gloria leaned into the aisle.

"What's going on?" Tessa felt a shiver of concern but quickly tamped down on it. The plane wasn't in the air, so it wasn't like a crash was imminent.

"I'm not sure." Gloria craned her neck.

Murmurs made their way from the front of the plane back through the aisle like a ripple through water. Tessa heard the word dead.

Someone died? She tried to boost herself up to see over the seat in front of her, but the people there were also straining to see, blocking the view.

"Who is it?"

"It's Art." Gloria's tone was hushed. "He's dead. That's strange. I didn't see his soul. Did you?"

Tessa shook her head, scanning every inch of air for a portal to the other side.

Art. The reaper from Minnesota with a flare for the artistic? Tessa hadn't even really met him, but she felt a pang of loss. He'd sounded like a nice guy. "I wonder who took him over," she said. Of course, any humans on the plane wouldn't have been able to see Art's spirit leave his body or the reaper who would have opened a portal to the other side. But any of the reapers on the plane surely could have.

"How did we miss it?" she asked.

"I'm not sure." Gloria looked troubled, but she shook her head and the expression cleared. "But it isn't like we can just shout up there and ask who crossed Art over. We'll have to wait until we get to the conference and ask around."

Tessa nodded. She settled back into the chair, aware that it would take longer for them to get airborne now. Art's body would need to removed from the plane. "Do you think he had a heart attack or something?"

"I don't know. Maybe." Gloria didn't look convinced.

As Tessa watched an ambulance squeal to a stop next to the plane and several EMTs race up the stairs, she wondered about the reaper who'd taken Art. Had he or she known about the assignment for a while? Like, while all the reapers were in the pub drinking and telling stories?

It was one thing to take the souls of strangers to the other side. Even that was sad sometimes. But how would it feel to take someone you knew? A friend or co-worker?

Tessa was pretty sure she didn't want to find out.

Chapter 5

Their decision to bring only carry-ons proved to be a good one. As Tessa and Gloria passed the luggage claim area, it was clear it would have taken them a while to deal with it. As it was, there was a line of reapers and regular folk pushing and shoving to get close enough to grab their bags.

Tessa's curiosity threatened to get the better of her. She wanted to talk to the reapers and see if she could find out more about Art's death. But there were lots of non-reapers around. It wasn't the right time or place.

Nor was it her job. But these days, Tessa found she often questioned the how, the why, and the timing of every death she heard or read about. Differentiating business from literal life and death was something easier said than done. She hoped there was a talk at the conference to cover such matters.

As they made their way to the rental car plaza, Gloria seemed unfazed. She chattered about what type of food to indulge in for their first night at the resort. Tessa's mind was only half on the conversation. It kept drifting to Art and what had happened to him on the plane.

Had there been a reaper waiting to escort him over?

Tessa knew from her training that there were circumstances under which someone could die without an assignment having been put in for them at a reaper agency. It was rare, but with the fact that humans had free will, choices could be made in a split second that the universe didn't seem to foresee. When it did happen, the soul wandered until a reaper could find it and properly escort it over.

She'd even heard whispers about a task force made up of specially trained reapers whose sole job it was to find such lost spirits. Of course, needing to call them in created a bunch of red tape for the agency. Meetings upon meetings. Retraining. Reprimands. This was why Cheryl had hesitated to do it when Tessa lost a soul, preferring to browbeat Tessa into finding him herself first.

Fingers snapping in front of her face drew Tessa out of the reverie. Gloria's well-manicured eyebrows were up. "Earth to Tessa Randolph. Are you in there? I was asking whether you like sushi. I know it's somewhat of an acquired taste. There's a good place close to our hotel that I forgot about. Last year, some of the other reapers and I ate there four times. It's that good."

Tessa's stomach growled at the thought. "Yum. Let's do it." There was no good sushi in Mist River. In fact, many small towns in Michigan lacked that particular delicacy, and Tessa loved it.

"Decision made!" Gloria gave a little fist-pump as they entered a large room dotted with rental car kiosks. "Hey! That's a familiar face a long way from home. Isn't that your hottie landlord?"

Tessa followed her friend's gaze and found Silas's smiling face as he exited the line of a competing rental car agency. She was a little surprised Gloria recognized him—she'd only met him once briefly when she came over to watch movies with Tessa and Abi. But she'd immediately honed in on Tessa's interest in Silas. In true close girlfriend fashion, Gloria had instantly made it her mission to tease Tessa about having a crush every chance she got.

"I wondered if I'd see you here—I didn't know which flight you'd be on." Silas held a set of car keys in one hand and carried a navy-blue duffel bag in the other. He wore khaki cargo shorts and a bright blue T-shirt.

He looked vacation ready and oh, so good.

"Hey," she managed to respond. "You're here!"

"I'm here." He shrugged. "I decided to just go for it, ya know?"

"That's great." It was great. Tessa's heart told her as much as it thumped louder and faster in her chest. Silas had come at her encouragement. But now that she saw him here, she wasn't sure what to do.

"I'm staying at the Roundtree Resort and Spa. Your hotel—the one you suggested—was completely booked, but mine isn't too far away." He glanced at Gloria and included her in his thousand-watt smile. "I'm Silas. I don't know if you remember—"

"Oh, I remember." She smiled back and sent a wink in Tessa's direction. "What brings you here, Silas? Vacation?"

"At Tessa's encouragement, yeah. I haven't had a vacation in so long that I'm already wondering what to do with myself. Not sure I know how to relax and live in the moment."

"I find it's easier to do than you think," Gloria said.

"I don't know." He turned to Tessa. "I'm already worrying about Mrs. Cross' dental appointment in two days. I usually take her to that kind of stuff."

"Your cousin can handle all that," Tessa said. "Try to put it out of your mind and just chill."

He shrugged. "I'll try." He leaned closer and whispered, "I'm a little afraid I'm going to be bored with nothing to do and no one to talk to."

"Tessa's going to have *lots* of free time," Gloria offered. She ignored Tessa's wide-eyed, questioning look. "I've got more meetings than she does because I have to attend some of the advanced stuff, so she'll be looking for something to do too. You guys should hang out."

What the heck was she talking about? This was the first Tessa had heard about Gloria having to go to presentations Tessa didn't.

Was she lying? She had to be. But Gloria's grandpa, who'd taught her to play Blackjack, would have been proud. Her face didn't show her hand at all as she kept her gaze on Silas.

Tessa realized then that he was looking at her, expecting some sort of confirmation. She stammered, "I'll be available most evenings. It would be nice to hang out. Fun," she corrected.

Silas set down his bag and pushed hair out of his eyes. "Yeah? Awesome. How about tonight? Would you maybe want to grab a bite to eat with me and then go see some sights?"

She cut her eyes to Gloria, whose smile was so wide it reminded Tessa of the Cheshire Cat. The other reaper nodded at Tessa encouragingly, despite their earlier plans.

"Okay," Tessa agreed. "That sounds like fun. Let's do it."

"How about now? I'm starved."

"Go ahead," Gloria urged, even giving Tessa a tiny shove toward her landlord. "I'll get our rental car and take your luggage to the resort. Get us both checked in too. There aren't any presentations until tomorrow morning." Without waiting for an answer, she grabbed Tessa's suitcase and started off. Over her shoulder, she called, "Have fun, you two."

Silas picked up his duffel bag and started toward a nearby door. "I asked around a little bit and found out where the best Cuban food in town is. You up for that?"

Tessa followed him, glancing back at Gloria, who stood in line at one of the kiosks. She winked and gave Tessa two thumbs up and then made a shooing motion.

"It sounds good, but I'm not dressed for a fancy meal. I've got my traveling clothes on."

Silas glanced at her, his eyes taking in her stretchy black yoga capris and worn Detroit Lions shirt. "You look great. I'm sure this place doesn't have a dress code." He used the key fob to unlock a silver sedan and shoved his bag in the trunk before opening the passenger door for her.

"Maybe we could just drive around a little and see what looks good?" She got into the car, her stomach doing a little flip. Whether from hunger or nerves, she wasn't sure.

Why would she be nervous? She was just going to explore a new city with a friend. That's all. It certainly wasn't a date or anything. No matter how much Gloria had acted like a slightly insane matchmaker.

"That sounds like a great idea." Silas went around and got in his side. Soon, they were driving along the coast, both of their windows down so they could enjoy the salty ocean breeze.

"Everything is so colorful here," Tessa mused as they passed a group of turquoise, orange, and yellow-painted shops. "I've always loved the bright colors of ocean towns."

"Mist River Manor is going to be due for a paint job soon. Maybe we should consider Caribbean blue." Silas grinned. The breeze caught his hair and deposited it over one eye, where it seemed to live most of the time anyway. Suddenly, he pulled over and parked the car. "Do you mind if we walk the boardwalk for a bit? I really need to find a kiosk or shop selling sunglasses. I forgot to bring some."

"Sure. My legs could use a stretch after the plane ride."

They strolled on the boardwalk for an hour or so, ducking into shops and buying Silas' sunglasses. Tessa got a pair too, even though she'd brought some. She couldn't resist a huge, purple-rimmed pair with rhinestones on the corners.

The sun set as they watched from a deck jutting out from the boardwalk overlooking the beach. Then, Silas suddenly pointed at something a little further along. "Whatever that truck is selling, it smells amazing."

Tessa inhaled a deep breath and groaned. "Mexican," she said.

"Let's go." Silas grabbed Tessa's hand and pulled her along, almost jogging, until they stood in front of the truck's window perusing the menu. Then he darted a look at her and abruptly dropped the hand to push back his hair.

Tessa was sorry he'd let go.

They ordered empanadas and a basket of chips and salsa to share and picked a spot on the sand to sit and eat. They munched in silence, watching the waves and other beachgoers wander along.

"This is nice," Silas said when his food was gone. "And you didn't need to be dressed fancy or anything."

She laughed and popped the last bite of empanada into her mouth.

It *was* nice.

In fact, Tessa found herself wishing she got to spend all of the next few days with Silas. The thought of attending boring reaper presentations—the thought of death in general—was far away when he was around. Silas was so alive, so full of life and energy, that it made her want to be that way too.

Chapter 6

The spread outside the conference room entrance was insane. Tessa surveyed the first of two long tables. There were all kinds of breakfast foods to choose from. Of course, she gravitated toward the sweets. There were pastries galore as well as French toast stuffed with cream cheese and chocolate chip pancakes.

But thinking of her bathing suit, she settled for scrambled eggs and some sliced fruit. Next to her, Gloria grabbed a sampling of all the treats, ignoring anything that wasn't sweet—except bacon. Because bacon. She stacked several slices on her already loaded plate.

"These talks can be boring," she said, gesturing to Mount Sugar on her plate. "This keeps it interesting."

To Tessa, it looked more like Gloria would be comatose in about a half hour. She grabbed a cup of coffee from the coffee station—and reluctantly snatched a couple donut holes—before following her friend to sit at one of six or seven long tables facing a small stage with a podium.

Tessa stuck pretty close to Gloria. So far, she'd only met a few other reapers in the elevator and the lobby. And she'd tried to act cool. But the truth was it was all slightly intimidating.

Part of her mind was on Silas, wondering what he was doing with the day. He'd dropped her off at a decent hour the night before. Gloria had been in their hotel room, waiting to grill Tessa on how the night had gone. She'd struggled to hide the disappointment on her face, hearing it was just a walk on the beach and some food truck eats with no goodnight kiss.

Tessa might've forgotten to tell her friend about the brief moment when Silas had taken her hand. She was still unsure herself if it had really happened—and if it meant as much to him as it did her.

Gloria sat next to Shirley, the reaper from British Columbia, who sipped tea and smiled at them from behind the steaming cup.

Music began to play, and a countdown timer started on a screen above the stage, signaling to everyone that the program would begin shortly.

Gloria and Tessa dug into their food. Around a bite of Boston cream donut, Gloria said, "How's things in the great white north, Shirl?"

"Oh, just fine. Just fine. And Mist River is still standing, I take it?"

"It's as exciting as ever," Gloria confirmed before gulping some orange juice. She wiped her mouth with a napkin. "Luckily, our district covers a pretty big area, so we have plenty of chances to get out of our micro-town pretty often. Oh, this is Tessa Randolph. She's a rookie this year."

The woman gave Tessa a kind smile. "I remember when I first started. It's such an exciting time."

Exciting. That was definitely one way to explain Tessa's first week on the job.

"Make sure you take notes here—there are always lots of good tidbits and takeaways. And come to my talk later today. It's lighter than most. I'm doing one on the funniest reaps I've done in my several decades on the job." She chuckled. "I've had some real roll-on-the-floor fantastic times."

Gloria jerked her chin toward the conference room doorway, where April was just entering. "While Shirl's talks are fun, there are others that border on torture." She rolled her eyes and leaned closer to Tessa to whisper, "I challenge you not to fall asleep during April's afternoon sessions."

Tessa snorted. "Boring, huh?"

"Mind-numbingly." Gloria leaned back, getting Shirley's attention once more. "Do you know anything about Art's death?"

The elder reaper checked that no one nearby was listening and then said, "Just that it wasn't planned. There was no order for it and no reaper ready for his soul. But April isn't discussing it with anyone. It's an off-limits topic, I guess."

Gloria frowned.

Just then, April tapped the microphone at the front of the room to check if it was on. Everyone settled in and quieted down. The district supervisor looked much like she had when Tessa met her back in Michigan—she wore a different gray suit that matched her hair. Tessa wondered if she had them specially made. Did April have to send in a snippet of her hair to get the fabric dyed the exact right shade? Like taking in a sample of something to get some paint made to match?

"Welcome, everyone. Thank you for taking your reaper career seriously and being here to learn and grow." April beamed at the crowd. A smattering of clapping died out fast when only a few joined in. She didn't seem to care and continued promoting the merits of the conference and the reaper profession in general. Near the end of the speech, almost as though it were an afterthought, she gestured toward a man in the front row and introduced him as Lee Stuart, the supervisor for the western district.

Once the keynote speech was over—and Tessa had learned that Gloria really wasn't kidding about the nature of April's talks—Tessa and Gloria studied the schedules they'd been given at check-in. There were multiple presentations going on at the same times all day, so they'd have to pick and choose which to attend.

As much as Tessa wanted to stay close to Gloria so she'd have someone she knew nearby, it quickly became apparent that they should split up to get the most out of the conference.

Gloria wanted to attend talks like *The Most Incredible Reapers in History* and *Reap the Benefits of Your Job: IRA Strategies for Reapers.* But Tessa knew she should attend the more basic talks like *How to Stay in the Shadows* and *Fifteen Ways to Handle a Reluctant Reap.*

"You'll be fine," Gloria encouraged her. "I'll meet up with you at lunchtime. We can attend the last talk of the day together." She gave a little wave and hurried off to catch up with another reaper she'd spotted.

Tessa consulted her schedule again and then headed to room 101 for the talk about staying in the shadows. Sticking with the theme of the talk, she chose a seat at the back of the room and watched other reapers file in. She recognized Cynthia, the reaper from Chicago, who slumped into a chair near the door, looking as miserable as she had back in the airport bar.

The speaker was Bubba from Seattle, and he couldn't have a more polar opposite presentation style from April. He was as much a hoot as Gloria had made him out to be. In fact, by the end of the talk, Tessa was a hundred percent sure that the man was horrible at blending into the shadows, reaper or not. He seemed to love being the center of attention.

As everyone herded toward the door after the talk, Tessa gathered her things as quickly as possible, intending to catch Cynthia. She wanted to see if she could get any information out of the other reaper about the allocation problem Timothy had narrowed down to the Chicago office.

Cynthia had disappeared by the time Tessa left the room. She was nowhere to be seen in the hallway. Apparently, the woman knew how to move in the shadows better than Bubba.

Maybe she should give the talk next year.

Someone brushed against her, and Tessa mumbled, "Ope, sorry about that," in true midwestern fashion as she turned to look at the person who'd bumped her.

It was a man, about a foot taller than Tessa. His hair was so black it looked like it had been dipped in ink. In fact, it shone so much it appeared to be wet, flowing. It fell to his shoulders with just enough waviness to be interesting. He was dressed all in black, too, with dress pants and a polo shirt that looked high-end, tailored to fit his body in exactly the way that would best show off his long, lithe, runner's muscles.

Tessa brought her eyes up to meet his and had to stifle a gasp. His irises were the palest of blue, and for a second, Tessa could swear they were pulsing. It was jarring. Inhuman, somehow. He smiled, and it looked more predatory than friendly.

She took a step back.

He smiled wider. "Greetings, Theresa Randolph." He glanced over her shoulder at the room she'd just exited. "Did you learn to stay shadowed?"

"Oh. Um. Yes. Lots to think about from that talk. I . . . um." Why was she stammering like a schoolchild? Tessa forced herself to straighten and meet his eyes again. Wait—how did he know her name? "I'm sorry. I missed your name. Did we meet before?"

"I make it a point to learn the names of all the new reapers. But I don't want to make you late for the next presentation. You have a lot to learn." With that, he turned and stalked away. Without really noticing him, people skittered out of his way as he walked, leaving the middle of the hallway clear for the strange, tall man. It reminded Tessa of mice scattering before a cat.

She shook her head to clear it and checked the schedule to see where to go next. It took longer to shake off the strange cool feeling the man had left behind.

The rest of the day went by in a pleasant blur. Tessa and Gloria met up for lunch, which was a lovely all-you-can-eat buffet. Gloria introduced Tessa to more people. During the afternoon sessions, Tessa recognized more of the folks in the rooms than she didn't. She was starting to get her sea-legs, so to speak—feeling more comfortable in the reaper community.

Before she knew it, the time had come for the last talk of the day: *Accountable Accounting in Reaping*. Wow. Just the title alone sounded boring. And since the talk was being given by April, Tessa knew it would be hard to sit through without falling asleep. She opted for a late afternoon cup of coffee. It was cold and stale.

There were no other presentations at the same time, and the main conference room they'd started in that morning filled up with people again. This time, Gloria and Tessa sat near the front, sitting close to Lee Stuart.

Frantic movement caught her attention, and Tessa leaned forward to find Timothy a few seats down, smiling and waving to her. There was a big brown stain on the left breast pocket of his ill-fitting gray suit. "Hello, again."

Tessa smiled and waved back.

"I hope you're having a good time. For me, it's all work, work, work."

"It's been interesting so far."

He nodded energetically, before April tapped the microphone and began speaking, silencing the whole of the crowd. Timothy looked disappointed.

April started her talk by expressing her hope that everyone had enjoyed a day filled with learning and fun. "To close out the first day, we're going to talk about accounting in the reaper business. It's crucial that we be impeccable with our record-keeping." She shuffled papers on the lectern in front of her and then adjusted the microphone. "If the numbers aren't right, your branch may incur tremendous costs in hunting down the problem and making it right." She looked out into the crowd, pinning someone with her gaze. Tessa craned her neck to see who.

It was Cynthia. The reaper from Chicago shrank in her chair as though trying to sink through the floor into oblivion as dozens of eyes landed on her.

Tessa felt sorry for the poor woman and made a mental note to invite her to dinner or something during the next few days of the conference time. It really seemed like she could use a friend or two.

April continued, showing slides that explained how reaper accounting was managed. Each agency got its assignments and did the associated reaping. If the two numbers didn't match at the end of the month, there was a problem. It could happen either way—not enough souls were reaped as there were orders or more reaping had been done than was ordered.

Sometimes, it was a matter of lazy reporting, and the matter was easily reckoned. Other times, it wasn't so simple. If an agency's manager couldn't find and reconcile the discrepancy within one month, the area's supervisor was called in. After that, the district supervisor got involved. Eventually, the owner of the entire organization had to be consulted.

"And no one wants that," April assured everyone in the room. "Mr. Blade has more than enough to occupy his time without such nonsense."

Tessa wondered about the owner. She made a mental note to question Gloria about him.

April continued, droning on about accounting and staying accountable by maintaining impeccable records. "We all know the reaping is the exciting part and the paperwork is drudgery, but without it, our whole system falls apart. Some of you may think of this as just a job. But as far as I'm aware, ours is the only job with the fate of the universe at stake. All of this—" she gestured to the room, to the word outside— "would be destroyed if we truly lose a soul long-term. I hope that explains how important accounting is."

Tessa's hand shot into the air, surprising her. She hadn't meant to ask a question, but her arm seemed to have a mind of its own.

April cast a cool stare at her and seemed to consider ignoring Tessa. But she sighed and said, "Yes?"

"What happens if someone dies whose death wasn't ordered? How is it investigated and reconciled?" She was proud that her voice didn't quaver. There was no hint of the trepidation she felt in her chest at speaking out in front of all those people.

"We have folks within our organization whose sole job it is to research those deaths and bring the accounting in-line," April said flatly before turning back to point at the screen. "Now let's talk about . . ."

But Tessa cut her off, shocking herself further. Loud and clear, she said, "What about Art's death? Was his accounted for?"

Chapter 7

Slowly, April turned around. A muscle in her jaw twitched as though she were clenching her teeth.

Tessa sat straighter, refusing to be intimidated.

Gloria gave a snort that sounded like a cross between awe and amusement.

"If you *must* know," April said, "it was not accounted for." Had her eyes been equipped with lasers, Tessa's forehead would have a rather large hole through it. The look was obviously meant to shut down any further conversation.

Though she itched to ask more follow-up questions, Tessa heeded Gloria's warning elbow jab and clamped her lips together. But April's answer had started a murmuring among the reapers in the room. The supervisor's gaze flitted around, and she held up a hand. "Please, everyone. There's nothing to be concerned about. We already narrowed in on the problem, and we'll have it straightened out soon. Now. If we could continue my talk . . ."

April went back to her presentation, clicking through slides and reading them verbatim off the screen. She'd lost her audience and her spirit. She ended rather abruptly a few minutes later and didn't take any further questions, despite the last slide being labeled for Q & A. She stormed out of the room with Timothy trailing behind.

"I can't believe you did that." Gloria shook her head and giggled. "April looked fit to be tied."

"I just don't understand why she's hush-hush about Art's death. I mean, there are so many reapers here right now. Death is our business. And if one of our own goes unexpectedly . . . well, it's a problem."

"I agree with you there."

"Surely, someone knows something about what happened or could help figure it out. I mean, if accounting is so important, why would April want to keep it a secret?"

Gloria shrugged. "Probably to try and prevent Lee Stuart from finding out about it. The two of them have a competitive working relationship. Actually, the competitiveness leaks into their personal lives too. They're like ex-spouses. Makes me wonder if they dated a long time ago."

"Must've been a bad break-up." Tessa smiled. She grabbed her stuff and followed Gloria out of the conference room.

"Let's drop our things in the room and then get a drink," Gloria suggested.

"Sounds good to me." Actually, Tessa had a long list of things she should be doing instead. She could avail herself of the hotel's fitness room. She'd been sitting all day, and her muscles were screaming for some blood-pumping action. But that could wait for tomorrow, when she planned to get up earlier and work out before the presentations started—especially if she wanted Danishes and donut holes for breakfast. Her tummy gurgled at the thought.

And that was another reason a drink was a bad idea. She hadn't had any dinner. Then there was Silas. What was he up to today? Should she try to me up with him?

The first thing Tessa did in the hotel room was check her phone. She'd left it behind so she wouldn't be distracted by it during the conference. She texted Silas, just a quick check-in to see if he'd a good day, then checked her messages.

There was a voicemail from Abi. "Your cat is a menace. I left my sweatshirt in your apartment last night, and she shredded it. Now she's laying on it and won't let me near her. Don't ever ask me to watch her again. She's evil. Bring an exorcist and a bottle of wine when you come back."

Tessa rolled her eyes and made a mental note to buy Abi a replacement sweatshirt in the airport gift shop on the way home. That and a bottle of Pinot Noir should butter her up and make her forget the tortie's bad manners.

Just as Tessa was setting the phone back on the nightstand, it rang, startling her. She glanced at the screen and groaned. She thought about ignoring the call, but it would never work. Cheryl would find some way to get in contact with her. She might even call the hotel bar. How embarrassing would that be?

Reluctantly, Tessa slid her finger over the screen and put the phone to her ear. "Hi, Mom!" She made her voice as cheerful as possible in hopes of setting the tone for the call.

"Are you learning anything?" Cheryl's tone took over. All business.

"Oh, yeah. Loads. I can totally stay in the shadows with the best of 'em now." Tessa carried the phone across the room so she could look in the mirror while she talked.

"Good. Make sure you use those newfound skills during the rest of the conference. April isn't in the mood to have anything go wrong." Cheryl paused. "You're not rocking the boat there, are you?"

"Boat? What boat? I haven't seen a boat. We've been stuck at the hotel." Tessa scrunched her hair, trying to give it more bounce. It looked limp and lifeless. The water at the hotel was softer than at home. She really should have packed her root booster.

"I sent you there to learn, Theresa. Not play in Miami."

"You know, if they wanted to stick us somewhere to learn, Michigan would've been the perfect place."

"I can tell by your tone that you are rocking the boat!"

"Mom! I don't know anything about a boat. Things are going smoothly. You know, except for the dead reaper on the plane."

"Yes, well, I heard about that. Unfortunate situation. But it's none of your business, so stay out of it." Cheryl's tone didn't allow for any argument, so Tessa didn't make one. She bit her tongue and leaned forward to check her complexion more closely. Her hair might not be doing well, but her skin seemed to love the extra humidity in Florida. Maybe she should spend some time with her head over a humidifier every day back home.

"Theresa!"

Tessa jumped. She'd been so busy thinking about her beauty regimen she must have missed something important her mother said. "What?"

"I asked whether you're taking notes. I'd like you to do a presentation on everything you learned when you get back."

"A presentation? Why? Don't you know all this stuff already?" She crossed to sit on the bed. Gloria had disappeared into the bathroom after shooting Tessa a sympathetic look.

"Of course I do. I want to see what *you* are learning. If you write it down, you're more likely to remember it. And if you teach it—it's even more likely to sink in. Plus, it'd be great for the whole office."

"I'll remember," Tessa said. "It's not rocket science. It's stuff like, 'Wear dark clothes when you go to an assignment, so you're less likely to stand out and be noticed.' I think I can grok that, Mom." She was ready to get off the phone and completely regretted ever answering.

"Fine. But take notes anyway. And be prepared for your presentation next Monday. What about the other reapers? Are you making friends? I hope you aren't being awkward, Theresa." Cheryl sounded a bit anxious, like it was too much to hope that Tessa could be cool.

"What's that supposed to mean? I can handle the rare social interaction with a co-worker. I'm not that ridiculous." Tessa felt herself pouting like a kid and forced herself to stop. In high school, her mother never liked her friends. She preferred to think Tessa didn't have any. "You know I have friends, Mom. I know how to behave."

"Sure you do, dear. It's just a little reminder." She paused. "What are you up to tonight?"

"Gloria and I are going down to have a drink in a few minutes."

"Don't overdo it! You know how you get when you drink too much." Cheryl made a tsk noise.

Tessa didn't have any idea what her mother meant, but she was beyond ready for the conversation to be over, so she said, "Yeah. Okay. I'll be careful. Bye!"

"Goodbye. I'll call you tomorrow."

Great. Tessa knocked on the bathroom door. "I need that drink ten minutes ago."

Gloria came out wearing a knee-length, hot pink sundress. "Ready!"

"Wait. I can't go with you looking like that and me looking like this." Tessa glanced down at her business casual clothes. "Let me change."

Gloria shrugged. "Go for it. I'm not the one in a hurry." She plopped onto her bed and began to scroll on her phone.

Tessa changed quickly. Her sundress was less flashy but still pretty—butter yellow with cream lace fringe. Gloria nodded approvingly when she saw it.

They headed downstairs and made their way across the lobby into the hotel bar, which already contained a fair number of reapers. Many of them still wore the clothes they'd had on during the day's presentations, and Tessa wondered if they shouldn't have changed.

"I'll be right back. I want to say hi to Hugh from Indiana." Gloria took off before Tessa could respond.

Wonderful. Tessa looked around, feeling like a middle schooler trying to find someone to sit with in a packed lunchroom where all the cliques were already seated together.

She decided things would look better once she had a drink in her hand. Or, at least, she'd have something to do with herself that would be less awkward than just standing there with nothing to do and no one to talk to.

Maybe Mom has a point.

She ordered a whiskey sour, paid the bartender, and then looked up and down the bar. At the far end, she spotted Cynthia, sitting alone nursing a bottle of beer. Without taking the time to overthink it, Tessa moved to sit beside the other reaper. "Hi. I'm Tessa Randolph, from the Mist River agency." She stuck out her hand.

Cynthia took the offered hand, reluctantly, it seemed, and shook it. "Cynthia Crooks from Chicago," she said and cocked her head. "You must work with Gloria, then."

Tessa nodded.

"That's cool. She's fun."

"Yeah, she's been really helpful getting me on the right track." Tessa eyed the woman. "She actually helped me with an unfortunate situation I ran into on my second day on the job." Tessa was thinking on her feet, trying to create some common ground and perhaps get a bit of information out of Cynthia. "I actually lost a soul because I was late to a death."

Cynthia's eyebrows raised in interest. "Really? Did you find it?"

Tessa nodded. "Eventually. But I had to figure out who killed him and why he was running from me first. It was kind of a mess." She paused and then dove in, throwing caution to the wind. The warmth of the whisky sour in her belly felt like courage. "Has anything like that ever happen to you?"

Cynthia took a sip of beer and shook her head. "I guess I've been lucky so far."

"That's good. You know, I had kind of wondered if you may have lost a soul or something too. Like I did."

"What made you think that?"

Tessa shrugged. "Because you've been looking kind of sad so far on this trip, and I know April visited your office right before this." At Cynthia's surprised expression, she explained, "April was at my office before she went to Chicago."

"Well, you're partially right. I'm upset because April accused us—my branch, I mean—of messing with the accounting. She thinks one of us screwed up and we're all trying to cover for it."

"Obviously, you're not," Tessa said. "But are you sure no one in your office is?"

"I can't be. But April laid the blame on my shoulders. She said we're going to have to figure it out before the conference is over." Cynthia slumped further over the bar. "I can't lose this job. But I don't know how to prove we didn't do anything wrong."

Tessa understood. She wanted to help Cynthia but had no idea how. "I'm sure it'll get straightened out. I'll tell you what—I'll keep my ears open. If I hear anything that could help you, I'll let you know right away."

Cynthia smiled and looked hopeful for once. "Thanks. That's really nice of you. And welcome to the reaper community. I'm sorry I'm not more fun to be around right now."

Tessa waved off the apology. "It's understandable that you'd be distracted." She saw Gloria heading toward them. "Do you want to join us? We're just having a couple drinks, and then we'll probably head to the pool."

"For more drinks?" Cynthia guessed.

Laughing, Tessa nodded. "Probably."

"I'd like that. Thanks!"

Tessa thought of something. "Hey, one more work question before we focus on fun. Do you know who reaped Art's soul on the plane?"

She shook her head, attention already on Gloria, who'd just sat next to Tessa. "No, I didn't see his soul or the reaper who took him over. Sorry. To be honest, I was pretty focused on my own problems."

"I understand." Tessa sighed.

Gloria ordered them all another round. Tessa tried to focus on the conversation, which had turned sharply to a discussion about the latest episode of a popular reality show.

But her mind kept skipping around between the messed-up accounting that April was investigating and the mystery of Art's untimely death.

She studied her drink, wiping the condensation on the side of the cup with her thumb. She was so out of it that she failed to notice a familiar face sidled up at the bar beside them. At least until a familiar hand came out of nowhere and brushed her forearm softly.

She jerked out of her thoughts to find Silas beside her, smiling.

Chapter 8

"I hope you don't mind me just showing up like this. It's a short walk here from my hotel, and I figured by your text you were probably done for the day. Are you?" Silas looked like a bronze statue—almost too perfect to be real. How in the world had he managed to get such a great tan in one day? Florida and Silas were getting along well.

"Yes, she's done." Gloria shoved Tessa off the barstool and followed her down. "There's a free table over there—let's grab it." She led the way to a small round table but at the last minute, turned to Cynthia and said, "Oh, there's Lydia. You're friends with her, right? Would you mind introducing me?"

Cynthia shrugged. "Sure. But I thought you . . ."

In the blink of an eye, they were gone. Gloria had managed to wriggle them both away so that she could be alone with Silas. *Wow. She's good.* For the thousandth time in recent days, Tessa wondered why Gloria didn't have a boyfriend.

Silas settled into the chair across from Tessa. He slid his beer onto the table. "So, how was the first day of your conference?"

"Boring." The word slipped out of its own volition. "I mean, super interesting and informative." She winced and sipped her drink.

He chuckled. "I can't imagine presentations about life insurance would be too much fun. What do you talk about? All I can imagine is someone droning on about amortization. Wait, is that a thing in life insurance or savings accounts?"

"I think it's loans." Tessa giggled. "But I could very well have attended a talk about amortization today and not know it. I mainly doodled in my notebook and drank enough coffee to watch my hands tremor."

"Are you an artist?"

"I can draw a stick figure with the best of them. I just didn't want my head to thud on the table and draw everyone's attention."

Silas grinned and looked around. "It must be nice to be around so many colleagues, though. That's something I kind of miss with my job. Aside from the residents, it's just me. It's kind of hard to have inside jokes about work with yourself. You look like a loon laughing away at your own internal monologue."

"I can see that. But at least you do have people around."

"True. But they usually want me to fix something. I guess your customers are different. I can't imagine. It seems like a rather grim business."

"You have no idea." Tessa couldn't tell him that it was more than that. Her customers were on their last checkout. Ever. "How long have you been a landlord?"

Before he could answer, someone bumped into Tessa from behind. She craned her neck around to find Bubba looking sheepish. "Sorry. My first day using feet," he quipped. "Tessa, right? Out of Mist River?"

"That's me," she said.

"I saw you in my shadows presentation. I hope it was helpful."

"Yeah, it was great."

Tessa hoped the brief compliment would shut Bubba up. But he seemed bent on continuing. *Alcohol does have a way of doing that.*

"I mean, April assigned the topics and presenters. It's not really my strong suit. I kind of figure, by the time someone's within a few minutes of dying, what's the point of hiding, you know?" He took a sip of the light brown, iced drink in his hand—maybe a Long Island iced tea.

Loose lips sink ships. Tessa shot a quick look at Silas. His slightly narrowed eyes studied Bubba closely, letting her know he was trying to figure out what the guy was on about.

She tried to think fast. "Um. Yeah. Delivering a settlement to a beneficiary is both the best and worst part of our job, right?" She hoped her tone didn't reveal the floundering feeling she felt inside.

Confusion flitted across Bubba's face, almost mirroring Silas' from a moment before. "Settlement," he repeated.

"Yes. Being a life insurance agent is, like, long stretches of horrible boredom punctuated by moments of sheer terror, right?" She elbowed Bubba in the thigh and tipped her head a tiny bit toward Silas, hoping to get the message across to the other reaper.

Bubba's gaze jerked toward Silas and understanding swept over his features. "Oh, yeah." He shook his head. "Delivering the settlement. Best and worst part. Well, I'll see you later. Enjoy the rest of the conference."

In his hurry to get away, Bubba tripped over his own feet and crashed into another table, spilling his drink all over the table where Gloria, Cynthia, and Lydia were seated beside Lee Stuart.

Cynthia looked as uncomfortable as ever, especially with the stain now covering her blouse.

But the western district supervisor threw a few napkins over the mess, handing a couple to her. "Bubba," he said jovially. "I believe this means you're cut off."

Tessa cringed. Poor Bubba. She felt a little responsible for that.

She returned her attention to Silas. "I guess some people started drinking earlier than others."

"Yeah. Wow. That seemed like a pretty morbid presentation you had to attend." A hint of confusion—no, it looked like actual suspicion—still floated behind his eyes.

"Well, like you said before, when you're a life insurance agent, you basically think and talk about death and dying all day long. I guess it starts to become second nature. I think the more experienced agents tend to forget that not everyone lives hand-in-hand with death all the time." She held her breath, hoping he bought her explanation.

Silas' shoulders relaxed and he took a swig of beer. "I can see that. There are some professions where a dark sense of humor is probably essential to handling the work. Could you imagine being a grave digger?"

"No." Tessa smiled, relieved that he seemed to have accepted her explanation.

"Or a medical examiner. Or, get this, a grim reaper?" He laughed, and Tessa feigned laughing alongside him. She made a mental note to suggest to someone a new presentation topic for next year's conference: *100 Ways to Hide Your True Career.*

Behind her, Tessa could hear a small group of reapers getting louder. One of them was telling a story about a funny reap she'd done. Tessa shot to her feet. This place was feeling awfully crowded. And it wasn't the drink making her throat close up.

"Do you want to get out of here?" she asked loudly, attempting to drown out the reapers and their stories. "I do. I've been in this hotel all day." There was no way she was going to be able to keep Silas from hearing something he shouldn't in a bar full of reapers drinking and getting loud.

Silas threw down the last of his beer and got up. "How about a walk on the beach?"

"That sounds great." Relief seeped into her mind, calming it, as they exited the bar and made for the front door.

"It's a nice evening," Silas said once they were on the sand.

Tessa took in the scene. The sun was beginning to set, casting a glittery reflection on the ocean, which was calm—only tiny waves lapped at the shore, making a faint tinkling sound. She took off her shoes and got close enough to the water to get her toes wet. "It's perfect," she agreed.

"I spent most of the day on the beach, but it's better with you." Silas looked at his feet instead of making eye contact.

She was glad about that because she could feel heat in her cheeks—a much better feeling than she'd had in the bar. "Beach life is nice, huh?"

He nodded. "I haven't been able to spend a lot of time like this in my life."

"Didn't you get to take many vacations when you were a kid?" Tessa's parents had made it a point to take a family vacation somewhere warm every February. That was the time of year when most Michiganders were well and truly tired of winter dreariness.

"I can't remember going on any," he answered. "We didn't have the money to do stuff like that." He glanced at her and then looked right back down. "My dad left when I was six. There were four of us little kids for Mom to feed and clothe. She did a fantastic job. I never needed something I didn't have. But there weren't a lot of extras. No sandy beaches or Mickey Mouse."

"That's understandable." She felt a stab of guilt. Sometimes, it was easy to forget how good you had it.

"Once my older brother, Liam, turned sixteen, he got a job, and that made things a little easier. In fact, I was able to join Little League. And Liam bought me a bat."

"Baseball," she said. "My dad loved baseball."

"Me, too."

"Did you play?"

The moonlight glinted off his gentle smile. "Something like that."

"Come on," she teased him, "what does that even mean?"

"Well, I didn't have anybody at home to practice with, but I spent every minute I could over at the ball field, talking anybody who wandered past into throwing for me for a few minutes. Mostly, I just threw the ball at the fence. Wore out this little section, perfecting my pitches."

"And?"

"I was pretty good. High school all-star and all that. I wanted to make a career out of it. Make the big bucks and get my whole family a big house and fancy cars." He snorted. "A kid's ridiculous dream."

Tessa's heart squeezed as she imagined young Silas spending hours on the ball field, late into the night, trying to get good enough to lift his family out of poverty. "I think it's a beautiful dream."

His head snapped up and he met her gaze with a wide-eyed one. "It didn't work out, though. I made it to the minor leagues but blew out my shoulder before I could get to the majors." He shook his head. "I should have spent that time studying computer science or something. Maybe it would have worked out better."

She wanted to say something smart, but nothing came to mind. She stared at the water instead.

"My family's doing fine, though," he said in a more cheerful tone. "Liam worked his way up to management and now he owns a little grocery store. My younger sisters both went into the medical field. My mom has a nice house in the suburbs, and she doesn't have to worry about anything. We all help take care of her. She deserves it."

That must be why he worked so hard. Silas knew what it was like to not have enough.

"Wow, I can't believe I just told you all that. Way to go, Si—you managed to be more boring than the woman's life insurance presentations." He snorted and shook his head again. "Sorry about that. I don't know what got into me. I don't talk about myself all that much. I promise."

"It's not boring," she insisted. "I'm glad you told me about it. I'd love to meet your family some day." *Oh, geez, Tessa. You basically just invited yourself to be his girlfriend.*

He stopped suddenly in the sand, grabbed her hand, and looked into her face. "I'd like that too," he said with a smile. "Tessa?"

"Yes?" She felt her body leaning toward his, anticipating a kiss.

His expression was earnest, and he leaned forward a bit too. "Do you want to find that empanada truck again?"

Chapter 9

"You look like something that cat of yours swallowed, partly digested, and then brought back up." Gloria's head tipped as she evaluated Tessa.

"Thanks. I appreciate your candor." Tessa rubbed her face and then ran a hand through tangled hair. "I'm going to hop in the shower."

"You don't look in any state to hop. How late were you out last night?" Gloria perched on the edge of her bed, already dressed for the conference in khaki capris and a scarlet scoop-neck blouse. "Thankfully, I didn't hear you come in—or else you'd have other problems this morning." She smiled.

Tessa groaned as she pawed through her suitcase for an outfit. "I don't know. Two or maybe three in the morning, I think."

"And you were with hottie landlord that *whole* time?"

"We lost track of time. We found this great food truck. But last night, it was parked next to a margarita truck. I'm not even kidding. Then we went for a walk and got hungry again."

"Not a good sign."

"Yeah, we found a little restaurant with a patio facing the ocean and had appetizers and drinks. There was a band. Some very bad dancing—on my part. Silas, it turns out, is an excellent dancer." She groaned again. "I missed my alarm this morning, too exhausted to get up and do my workout. I guess I'm too old to stay up past midnight."

Gloria snorted. "Okay, Cinderella." She grinned. "At least you got to spend some quality time with your prince."

"He's not my prince." She went into the bathroom and shut the door.

Through it, Gloria's voice floated. "Stop fighting it! You two are adorable together. Like Ken and Barbie. William and Kate. Beauty and the Beast." She paused. "You know, after the Beast got un-furry."

"I don't see how I could date someone right now. He's already gotten suspicious a couple of times, I think. You know, about the reaper thing." Tessa turned on the water, drowning out whatever Gloria may have responded with.

It was her argument and she was going to stick to it. There was just no way that she and Silas would work. Their lives were so different. And once they were back in Mist River, everything would go back to normal. Wouldn't it?

When she came back out, dressed and ready to go, the other reaper acted like there hadn't been any interruption in their conversation. "Reapers date normal people. It *can* be done. You just have to get better at explaining away the weird. And, eventually, you could even tell him the truth. If you guys get serious and you're sure he'll keep the secret. He seems like the type that could."

"He is," Tessa agreed.

She pondered that as they headed for the breakfast buffet. Could she really date Silas and keep the true nature of her career under wraps? At least, until and unless they got serious enough for her to divulge the secret? Maybe she was overthinking it. Or maybe she was just crap at keeping secrets herself. It hadn't been easy at the bar. But then again, she wouldn't always be surrounded be several hundred other reapers.

She pushed away the questions, deciding they would be better examined when she wasn't so tired.

Tessa went straight for the coffee bar. The shower had perked her up a little, but she was counting on the caffeine blast to help her enter full-on human being mode.

"Lucky for you, it's a half day of talks." Gloria munched on a cream cheese-covered bagel. "Team building exercises this afternoon."

"That sounds like fun, I guess. As long as there's no sky-diving." She hadn't completely hated the jump she'd done with the Hansons, but Tessa still had no desire to make leaping out of planes a habit.

"There are some choices. Zip lines, snorkeling, stand-up paddle boarding . . . that's one I'm leaning toward."

"That sounds fun. As long as I've got my balance back by then. I feel a little unsteady still." Tessa's stomach growled, and she started loading a plate with fruit because everything else seemed too heavy.

Gloria nodded approvingly. "That should help."

By the time Tessa had finished eating, she was running late to the first presentation, *The Grim Reality of Social Media*. It was supposed to be about how to keep your reaper job secret in the age of cell phones and social media, and Tessa thought maybe it would give her some ideas about how to handle the situation with Silas.

There was only one empty chair in the small room when Tessa arrived, and she slid into it with a huff.

"You just made it," the man next to her leaned over to say with a wink.

Tessa realized it was Lee Stuart. He looked bright-eyed and ready to go, unlike her. The food and coffee had made Tessa feel better, but she still felt like another couple hours of sleep would be beneficial.

"Yeah. In the nick of time." She pulled out a notebook and pen and settled into the chair.

"This should be a good talk. Preston Peters, out of the LA office, is one of my best reapers. I'm sure he'll have some good tips to share." He eyed Tessa for a minute. "You're new, aren't you?"

"Yes. I'm from Mist River, Michigan."

He nodded. "Ah. One of Cheryl's crew." He paused, squinting as though trying to see something better. "I'd give you my condolences at having to work under her part of the organization, but I'm a gentleman, so I'll keep those thoughts to myself." He laughed at his own joke. "How are you enjoying the conference so far?"

"Oh, you know, I'm trying to soak up all the information I can. Just listening to all the more experienced reapers and all that. They're a wealth of knowledge. But I'm really looking forward to when I'm not the newbie anymore, when I can share some wisdom with somebody." She cast a sidelong glance at him, wondering if it was a good idea to say the next thing. With an internal shrug, she threw caution to the wind. "You know, someone mentioned to me that you and April have a friendly competition thing going on."

"Friendly. Yeah. Okay, we'll go with friendly." He smirked. "But it's not really a competition. It's April trying to keep up with me. She's always eating my dust."

Tessa had a feeling that was a gross exaggeration, but she nodded amicably. "She's probably distracted right now by the accounting glitch going on."

"She better fix it soon. Or I'll handily win the supervisor of the year award at the end of the conference. And this will be, what, the third year in a row. Not that I'm keeping track." He winked again.

"She thinks someone in the Chicago office screwed something up."

Lee scoffed. "April's just looking for a scapegoat. If there's been an accounting glitch, it came directly from her own office." He leaned closer to whisper, "Timothy is the brains between the two of them, but he's been known to make mistakes like this before."

"You think he made the accounting mistake? How? Did he forget to record some assignments?"

"Oh, I'm sure of it. He probably got distracted by a sci-fi marathon on late-night TV or something. Guy's a total geek. I'm more of a sports guy myself. Do you like sports?"

"Baseball," she said without thinking.

"America's pastime," Lee approved.

She wanted to ask more about the accounting issue, but Preston Peters tapped the microphone on his lapel, calling the presentation to order. She settled for doodling a picture of Timothy with a ketchup stain on his lapel during the talk, hoping for a chance to ask Lee more questions when it was over. But the supervisor got up before Preston finished talking, squeezed behind Tessa's chair, and left.

The next couple of hours dragged by with two more boring presentations, then Tessa met up with Gloria for lunch before the team-building exercises. They pored over the pamphlet that listed their choices as they munched on sandwiches and chips.

Tessa pointed to one that looked interesting to her. "How about we do this before the stand-up paddle board lesson?"

"An escape room?" Gloria considered for a moment and then shrugged. "Sure, why not? You feeling sharp enough to solve a mystery?"

Tessa chuckled. "I'm perfectly fine. The food and coffee helped, plus I basically slept through this morning's presentations with my eyes open. I'm going to try to get to bed early tonight, though."

"Good idea."

The escape room was set up in a dingy, out-of-the-way room in the hotel basement. Soon, Tessa was engrossed in the experience of solving a set of clues in order to find the key to unlock the door. Where usually, it was the whole group trying to escape the room, they'd made this into a competition to get out first. Gloria and Tessa partnered up against three other reaper pairs, including Bubba and Shirley, who turned out to be their biggest rivals.

In the end, Shirley figured it out moments before they did.

"Ha!" Bubba jabbed a finger at Tessa and Gloria. "You guys owe us a drink!"

Tessa laughed. "Okay, okay. I'll buy you a bottle of cheap domestic. But you have to promise us a rematch next year."

Gloria glanced at her watch. "We're going to have to hurry if we want to make it to the paddle board lesson." She pulled Tessa's arm.

They hurried out of the hotel, past the dock where a group was gathering for snorkeling, toward the designated meeting spot on the beach for the paddle board excursion. As they got closer, Tessa slowed down. April and Lee were there, along with Preston, Cynthia, and Timothy. She considered bolting and going snorkeling instead. Hanging out with the two district supervisors really didn't strike her as a good time. But Gloria grabbed her arm and kept marching forward.

Man, the woman really wanted to paddle board.

A man in board shorts and a rash guard scurried around, fitting people with lifejackets and boards and explaining the basics of stand-up paddle boarding. Timothy flitted around for a few minutes but then said, "Okay. Looks like you're in good hands, April. I'm going to head over and make sure everything's going well with the snorkeling contingency."

April ignored her assistant completely, and he left after an awkward silence.

If my boss was that mean, I'd be looking for a new job. Cheryl might be a little on the critical side and she had an annoying habit of using Tessa's full name, but she wasn't outright mean.

As she watched Timothy leave, a thought occurred to Tessa. Lee had said Timothy was the brains behind the operation at the eastern division's office. He himself had bragged to Tessa that he kept the accounting registers for the agencies in the district. Could he be behind Art's unaccounted for death somehow?

Tessa wouldn't blame him for wanting to make April look bad—she was horrible to him.

But she didn't have much time to ponder the thought because raised voices drew her attention. April and Lee faced off a few feet from each other. April's face was twisted in fury.

"Don't dish it if you can't take it, man. I'm only offering a standard bet—just like we always wager. Too scared to take it?"

Lee smirked. "When have I ever been afraid to take a bet with you?"

"Then what's the issue?"

"You haven't laid down fair terms. We're both beginners, so there has to be some leeway. I propose we each get a little practice time before we start the timer. Then, it's on. Whoever stays on longest wins."

April shrugged. "If *you* need a couple of free falls into the ocean, that's fine. It'll just give me time to get sea legs, so to speak. Does five minutes sound fair?"

"More than."

She smiled devilishly. "Then I'll be accepting my steak dinner voucher from you within five minutes' time. Let's go." She grabbed her paddle board and splashed into the water.

The instructor, alarm plastered over his bronze face, said, "Wait! I need to go over some basics first."

But April continued as though she hadn't heard him.

Lee gave a small shake of his head, picked up his board, and advanced more slowly into the surf.

The instructor brushed a hand through his sandy blond hair and appeared flummoxed. Finally, he grabbed his own board and waved an arm for the rest of the group to follow him. He began going over the basics of paddle boarding, speaking faster than Tessa believed he normally did.

April climbed on her board, stood up, and began to use the paddle to move forward. Lee watched for about half a second and then leaped onto his own board, taking only a moment to balance, and then he too advanced into the small waves.

"They're something else, aren't they?" Tessa said over her shoulder to Gloria.

But her friend didn't answer.

Tessa climbed onto her board, sitting with a leg thrown over each side, and twisted to see what was going on.

Gloria was in the water, clutching the paddle board like it was her only anchor in a stormy sea. Her face was slack, eyes wide. Tessa saw something in her friend she'd never seen before: fear.

Tessa bit back a laugh. The water couldn't be much calmer. It was suitable for toddlers, and they weren't out deep yet. "Hold onto the far side of the board and kick," she called. "That'll give you the momentum to get onto it."

Gloria maneuvered the paddle board slowly to the position Tessa recommended. She hoisted her body up, kicking madly, resembling nothing so much as a huge seal clambering up onto a rocky ledge.

This time, Tessa couldn't hold back the chuckle. "There you go. You got it." She popped up onto her feet and stood, balancing with the paddle in her hand. "Now, just get to the center of the board and stand up. It's not hard. Keep your center of gravity under you and just sort of . . . feel the water. Move with it."

Gloria shot her a look that clearly said what on earth are you babbling on about? She inched forward on her belly, trying to get closer to the center of the board. But she went too far and, before it was possible for her to do anything to stop herself, plunged head-first off the far edge of the board into the water.

Tessa laughed and used her paddle to turn back toward her friend. The rest of the group was further out, watching April and Lee compete for who could stay on their board the longest.

Gloria's head popped up, her life jacket helping her get upright. She sputtered, coughed, and splashed. "Argh," she cried.

Tessa paddled closer. "Are you okay?"

More sputtering was the only answer.

Then something caught Tessa's attention in the water near Gloria.

No. It couldn't be. There was no way.

Tessa, being from Michigan, had always felt safe in the water. There was no salt and there were no sharks or other crazy marine life that could kill you. You just had to respect the power of the Great Lakes. And the cold. They were always cold.

But that wasn't the case here. Here, the warm and clear waters harbored sharks.

And Tessa had never, ever expected to see one, but there it was—within a few feet of Gloria, its dorsal fin looking just like they did in movies. Until that moment, she hadn't even believed that was really a thing outside of *Jaws* and its many imitators.

For a moment, Tessa froze. She didn't know what to do. Should she shout, "Shark!" again, like they do in movies? Should she alert the instructor and everyone else?

It didn't take her long to dismiss that idea. It would only panic Gloria, and that probably wasn't the best idea. In fact, Tessa needed to get her friend to calm down and stop acting like a flopping fish in the water.

She maneuvered her paddle boat carefully between the shark and Gloria. Her heart pounded wildly, but Tessa ignored it, focusing only on the two beings in the water. Time seemed to slow down as she forced her breathing to calm. She told herself Gloria wasn't going to die. There was no reaper around, ready to escort her soul over the veil.

That was when she saw Lydia standing on the beach. She wasn't watching April's and Lee's antics. She was staring right at Gloria.

No. No, no, no, no.

Tessa spoke as calmly as possible but infused her tone with authority. "Gloria. Stop splashing now. There's a problem, and I need you to do what I say."

The other reaper looked at Tessa's face. She must have seen something there because she stilled.

"Okay. Grab the far side of paddleboard with both hands. Pull it toward yourself and then kick . . . calmly . . . to get yourself up. Do it now."

Gloria did what Tessa said, and Tessa glanced at the shark. It seemed to have stopped swimming and was just sort of hovering there, as though it were watching. Waiting.

Tessa gulped and turned her attention back to Gloria, who was about halfway onto the paddle board. Tessa glanced at the shore.

Lydia was gone.

By the time she looked back, Gloria was on her knees on the board.

The shark's fin changed directions and the creature sped off, toward the dock.

Tessa blew out a breath. "Hey, what do you say we head to shore? I think I'm done paddle boarding."

"I'm with you." Gloria didn't stand up. She used her hands to doggy paddle her way back to the sand.

They got out of the water, and Gloria laid on her back on the beach, panting and staring at the sky. Her black hair was matted to her head, drenched.

Tessa giggled and sat next to her friend.

"How come you're so good at that and I'm so horrible?" Gloria grumbled.

Tessa shrugged. "I have no idea. But it was fun! Thanks for insisting on it." Okay, it hadn't actually been fun. But Tessa didn't think Gloria really needed to know about the shark. "Let's put our gear away."

They both got up and carried their paddle boards back to the small building.

Gloria sighed, "Honestly, I was hoping my hair wouldn't get wet or else we'd have gone snorkeling. Now, I need to go back to the room and get changed and redo my hair."

As they approached the dock in front of the hotel, Tessa realized something was going on. An ambulance, silent but with lights flashing, was parked as close to the water as possible, and a crowd had gathered around it. For as many people as were there, the atmosphere was almost dead quiet. It felt eerie.

Tessa and Gloria stood on tiptoes at the back of the crowd, craning their necks to get a glimpse of what was going on. In front of them, people silently shifted, letting the two women maneuver their way through. In fact, it seemed as though many people were easing away from the scene.

When they got to a clear spot, Tessa immediately knew why people would be get away.

There was blood all over the dock and in the water.

She heard the word *shark* filter through the crowd. A few reapers stood dripping water, towels wrapped around them, snorkels and masks pushed onto their heads. Everywhere, there were pale, shocked faces.

Tessa forced herself to look at the injured person the EMTs were working on. It was clear their efforts would be fruitless—no one could survive injuries like that. It had to be the same shark she'd seen. The one that had considered attacking Gloria. It must have found easier prey by the dock.

"Who is it?" she whispered, straining to see something that would help her identify the dead reaper.

Gloria, also a degree paler than usual, gave her a wide-eyed look and whispered back, "It's Cynthia."

Chapter 10

Tessa and Gloria retreated from the front of the crowd, slipping past other reapers. Near the back, they found Bubba, standing with his arms crossed. He wore swim trunks and dripped onto the grass. For once, his expression wasn't joyful.

"What happened?" Gloria asked.

He grimaced. "Shark attack."

"We got *that* much." Gloria glared at him.

"I'm wondering who took her over?" Tessa said.

"I didn't see anyone do it." Bubba shrugged and shook his head. "Terrible way to go."

Tessa agreed with the other reaper's sentiments, but her attention was captured by someone else. She elbowed Gloria and nodded toward Timothy, who was just leaving the dock. He looked like the poster boy for a *Casper* movie trailer—his face was so pale it seemed incompatible with being alive.

Tessa whispered to Gloria, "Did you see that? Timothy looked rattled."

Gloria's eyes tracked Timothy's back as he headed for the hotel. "He looks shaken, for sure."

Tessa went to ask Bubba if he'd seen Timothy at the scene, but his back was turned as he spoke to Preston in hushed tones.

She quizzed Gloria with her query instead. "Do you think he had something to do with it?"

"He's not a reaper. He's a numbers guy. Sure, he's around reapers a lot and deals with death, but only on the periphery.

I don't think he has much cause to be up-front-and-center like us. He's probably freaked out at the sight of all the blood. Plus, he knew Cynthia. A little bit, anyway. It's possible he's never seen anyone die before." She glanced back toward the horrible scene. "Especially so violently."

"You're probably right." Tessa chewed her bottom lip, thinking about how Timothy had seemed in a hurry to leave the paddle board area and get to the snorkeling session. It didn't make sense. Sure, he was a numbers guys. An allocations guy, to be exactl. And allocations meant death.

But why would he do that? And, assuming Art's death had been arranged by the same person as Cynthia's, what would Timothy's motive have been?

The EMTs got Cynthia's body into the ambulance, and the vehicle left without its flashers or sirens on. The crowd on the dock dissipated, everyone going off in separate directions, moving slowly.

When they were finally back in the hotel lobby, Gloria said, "Want to get a drink?"

Tessa shook her head. "I don't think so. I'm not really feeling it."

"You're right." Gloria sighed. "Going to the bar right now is a bad idea. Tell you what. How about we head back to the room and order room service on the company card?" She waggled her eyebrows.

Tessa blinked. "Company card? What are you talking about?"

"Oops." Gloria winced. "I figured Cheryl gave you one too." She pulled a black credit card out of her back pocket and waved it under Tessa's nose. "I keep it close in case I get hungry.

And I'm always hungry. We get to comp our food while we're here. I thought you knew."

Through gritted teeth, Tessa said, "No. She didn't give me one of those."

She thought of Silas using Mrs. Cross' money to buy expensive meals for them—money he could be saving for less expensive meals out with her when they got back home. Only, Tessa wasn't ready to think about what they were going to be when they were back home. She wanted to live in the here and now. After all, not every day was guaranteed. Just ask Cynthia.

"Can I borrow that tomorrow?" she asked. "I think Silas and I need to go on a dining spree. I'm feeling a little ravenous from all the learning I've been doing."

Gloria dissolved into giggles. "You're going to get me fired. But yeah, you can borrow it. Anything to help you two lovebirds realize you're perfect for each other."

They headed for the elevator. "Why don't you spend as much time focused on your own love life as you do mine?"

Gloria gave her a sidelong look and a mischievous grin. "Maybe I do."

Tessa's jaw dropped for a second, then she scowled at her friend. "Oh, I see how it is. You get to keep your cards close to the vest to avoid my input but, in the meantime, you just carry on with all your delightful commentary about my love live? I mean, about my *friendship* with Silas."

Gloria shook her head as they got on the elevator. "Nah, I'm kidding. I'm not dating anyone right now. Just living vicariously through you. The meet-cute is the best part. But as soon as I'm interested in someone, I'll let you know."

Tessa's phone buzzed. She pulled it out of her pocket to find a text from Abi: *Your evil cat left a hairball for me to step on in the kitchen. Then she looked smug. Have I said to get a new cat-sitter next time? If not, I'm saying it.*

Tessa texted back: *That's how she shows love. You are her chosen one—forever and always Pepper's cat sitter.*

A second later, Abi replied: *Promise you'll bring home wine AND chocolate if you want me to even consider not strangling this creature.*

Chuckling, Tessa shook her head and texted back: *I will bring payment. Unless . . . Pepper beats me to it.*

What does that even mean? Does she bring you mice? Am I going to find a mouse? Tessa? Really???

Have fun! Xoxo

As they entered the hotel room, Gloria said, "Weren't you supposed to hang out with Silas tonight?"

Tessa flopped onto the bed and threw an arm over her eyes in her best impression of Scarlet O'Hara. "Yes. But I don't think I'm up for it. I just want to watch a funny movie and eat until my sides burst."

"I'm already on that second part." Gloria waved the room service menu in the air and picked up the room phone to place an order.

Tessa sat up and scrolled on her phone until she found Silas' name. She tapped it and waited for him to answer.

"Hey! Done with the team-building stuff already?"

"Yes." She winced. "But it ended kind of badly. One of our agents was killed in a shark attack."

She heard him suck in a breath. "That's . . . pretty terrible and not at all what I expected you to say. Wow. How are you holding up?"

"Okay, I guess. But would you blame me if I'm not really up for going out tonight? Is that all right with you?" She held her breath, hoping he wouldn't be too disappointed.

"Oh, yeah, sure. Actually, that works out fine because I had a little incident today myself. I could use some rest."

"Incident? What incident?" She felt a twang of alarm.

"Jellyfish sting. And, no, I didn't do that thing they say to do to make jellyfish stings feel better. I was on a crowded beach. And I don't know yoga."

"How bad is it?"

"It's pretty swollen. I took a bunch of Ibuprofen and I think I'm going to crash early."

Tessa blew out a breath. "Okay. Well, I hope you feel better. Talk to you tomorrow."

They hung up, and Tessa sprawled out on the bed. Gloria had turned on the TV before going into the bathroom. Tessa stared at the ceiling and thought again about how Timothy had looked when he'd retreated from the dock.

But before she had much time to think about it, there was a knock on the door. She dragged herself off the bed and opened it to find a bellhop with a cart so loaded with food it was fairly he'd managed to push it without losing a bunch. There were appetizers, steaks, seafood, a whole chocolate cake, and milkshakes—the kind that come in glasses with a mound of whipped cream and a cherry on top.

Good grief.

Gloria really knew how to leverage a spending account.

Chapter 11

"Today's sessions are canceled." April's face revealed more lines than usual, as if she'd stayed up all night after Cynthia's death. She paused, pursing her lips for a few seconds before continuing. "Our thoughts and condolences are with Cynthia's family during this difficult time."

They were in the main conference room. It was only about half full. Many of the other reapers must've known this was coming and had chosen to sleep in. But the caterer hadn't gotten the memo. Tessa guiltily pushed away her plate, piled high with breakfast food. After gorging themselves on room service, and with the thought of Cynthia's death back on her mind, she was in no mood to eat.

She only wished April was more forthcoming with information. Surely, this wasn't planned. And none of the reapers who had been snorkeling seemed to have seen much, including her soul or anyone taking her to the other side.

April cleared her throat. "We need everyone to stay on-site and be prepared for questioning as we investigate these strange occurrences." Without a proper closing, April left the stage and the dull roar of conversation rose in the room.

Gloria, with the metabolism of a hummingbird and apparently not plagued with the same stomach-turning visions as Tessa, spoke around a mouthful of sausage. "Well, I guess we're stuck here for the day. What are you going to do?"

Tessa shrugged. "There's not much *to* do."

"Let's see." Gloria quirked her lips in mock thought. "Since I'm living vicariously through you. I say you invite hottie landlord to hang out at the pool." Gloria grinned and popped a grape into her mouth. "Besides, your tan could use some work."

Tessa raised an eyebrow.

"What? Dragon-lady didn't say we couldn't have visitors. She just said we couldn't leave. I'm going to book myself a full day at the spa upstairs. So, if they want to question me—they'll have to find me first."

"A spa day does sound good . . ."

"You are not invited. Again, if I were in your shoes, I'd be with that hottie. I'm only taking the second-best option so that you and he can be alone. I'm not a third wheel." A sly grin spread across her face.

"Fine." Tessa pulled her plate back, her growling stomach, having valiantly fought off the nausea, now demanded sustenance. "Anyway, I wouldn't want Silas to find out I had a whole day off and didn't call him. After all, he's only in Miami because I suggested it."

"Atta girl." Gloria bumped Tessa's shoulder with her own. "You two are perfect for each other. So, stop being all . . . Tessa . . . and catch that hunk o' man, already."

"The problem is I can never stop being Tessa." She gave up the pipe dream of a healthy breakfast and started in on a cruller.

"Well, you can be Tessa, but just don't be *that* Tessa."

The aforementioned Tessa narrowed her eyes. "Which Tessa would that be again?"

"The one who overthinks everything. Be spontaneous Tessa instead."

"That's ridiculous. Besides, I used to be spontaneous, and that's how I ended up with Frank."

"That's a story you're gonna have to tell me someday."

"I'd prefer not to."

"Then write a new story. A better one." Gloria didn't say any more. She just grinned, winked, and stuffed some toast with jam in her mouth.

After breakfast, Tessa texted Silas. He responded almost immediately, letting her know he needed to change but would come right over after that.

With a little flutter of nerves in her belly, Tessa got into her suit and headed to the pool. It was outdoors, with palm trees lining the edges of the blue and green-tiled deck. The water glistened invitingly.

There was a smattering of people there, mostly other reapers, who Tessa avoided. She found a small empty table with an umbrella to put her bag on, then settled into a lounge chair next to it. She leaned back, closed her eyes, and let the sun soak into her skin.

"Is this chair taken?"

Tessa's eyes popped open. She expected to see Silas—to hear Silas's voice—but instead, her heart sped up when she recognized the tall man she'd seen in the hallway on the first day of the conference.

He wore black swim trunks, and his dark, shoulder-length hair was now caught up in a black leather band. The man looked like he'd never eaten a carb in his life. She was glad dark sunglasses hid his strange eyes.

Tessa realized too much time had gone by since he'd asked about the lounge chair next to her. "No. I mean yes. Um, actually, my friend is coming in a few minutes," she stammered.

He smiled, revealing those predatory teeth, and lowered himself into the chair without acknowledging what she'd said. He leaned back and smiled. "Ah. This is the life, is it not?"

What an odd speech pattern. Like he was European or something. Or straight out of a Victorian romance novel. "Y . . . yes. It's really nice. Are you here for the conference?" The guy did give off subtle reaper vibes, but she hadn't seen him attending any of the presentations or in the buffet lines.

He glanced her way and then returned to facing the sun. "I'm here to *observe* the conference, yes. Mainly, I am enjoying cocktails and surfing. There were some gnarly waves yesterday."

Tessa felt her eyebrows rise. She wouldn't have pegged him as a surfer dude. "I think I missed your name before. I'm Tessa." He'd already demonstrated he knew that, of course, but her midwestern politeness didn't care.

"My name is Corwin Blade." His fingers laced over cut abdomen muscles.

Blade. She'd heard that name recently. Where was it?

"Nice to meet you, Corwin." She tried to watch him without being obvious about it. The man had such an unusual energy about him. If she had to explain it, the word she'd choose would be *ancient*. But that was crazy. The guy didn't look a day over thirty.

"And Tessa, how are you enjoying your new job?"

"It's great. Except for the fact that my co-workers seem to be dying disproportionately." She winced, not sure that was a proper topic of conversation. But she couldn't help herself. "Do you know anything about that? About poor Cynthia or Art? April says their deaths are unaccounted for."

He waved a hand. "I gave up on handling the mundane details of reaper work a long . . . long time ago." He tipped his head to look at her.

It was a bit disconcerting not to be able to see his eyes through the dark glasses. But Tessa knew from experience that being able to see them was just as unnerving.

"Oh, are you retired or something?" As soon as she said it, Tessa knew that was ridiculous. Corwin Blade was nowhere near retirement age.

He chuckled, and the sound reminded her inexplicably of metal gears grinding. A shiver skittered up her spine, and she glanced around to make sure there were still people nearby. No one was sparing a glance in their direction.

"I guess you could say I'm retired, yes. I've delegated all my responsibilities to others. I serve in a much more advisory capacity now. But, if necessary, I'll step in and handle this current situation." He returned his head to a straight position. "It's not likely that I'll need to, though. My people are quite capable. Especially the head of the task force on unaccounted-for deaths. Top-notch, that one. A real go-getter."

"That's good. I guess." Tessa threw her legs over the side of the lounger, deciding it was time to put some distance between herself and the strange man. "It was nice meeting you. I think I'm going to get a drink from the bar."

He wiggled his fingers in a cutesy wave. "Have fun."

Tessa grabbed her bag and took a few steps before his voice stopped her.

"One more thing." His words lingered in ears. "Should you ever need it, the power of the Scythe is always within your grasp. You need only call for it."

She turned back toward the chairs, but Blade was no longer on his lounger. He was standing a couple of inches away from her. She forced herself not to shriek or jump backward. "The . . . Scythe?"

"It's my strongest power. And sometimes I loan it out to people who work for me. But only those who are the most promising. The smartest. Reapers with the greatest of potential." He grinned. "Like you."

Slowly, as though the gears in her brain were grinding, his words made sense. "You're . . ."

"I'm late for a date with a fine young lady and a coconut-flavored drink," he finished. "Have a lovely day, Tessa Randolph. And remember what I said about the Scythe." He saluted with the tip of his finger on his sunglasses and then strode across the pool deck toward the hotel, brushing past Silas as he went.

Silas rubbed his arm but didn't look at Blade. He spotted Tessa, smiled, and walked over to her. "Hey! Sorry it took me so long. I got locked out of my hotel room and had to get them to make me a new pass key." His eyes moved down to her feet and back up to her eyes. He swallowed hard. "You look . . . I mean you look . . . wow."

"Thanks," she barely acknowledged the compliment. Her eyes were still on Blade's back. "That man has a strange energy, doesn't he?"

Silas' gaze followed hers, and then his brow furrowed. He looked back at her. "What man?"

"The one I was talking to just now." She took in Silas' bewildered expression and realized the truth too late. Her landlord hadn't been able to see Blade. She waved a hand.

"Never mind. I guess he slipped into the changing room. I'm sure he was gone before you came out onto the deck." She smiled. "I was just going to get a cocktail. Do you want one?"

His face smoothed, and he grinned back at her. "Something coconutty sounds nice."

"Yeah. They have that. It's called a piña colada."

"I'll take one for each hand." He smiled.

As they headed toward the pool bar, Tessa glanced at the door Blade had disappeared through. She had no further doubt about the man's identity, but she couldn't help but feel a little concerned about his motives.

Why had the original Grim Reaper taken a special interest in her?

Chapter 12

She ignored the buzzing purse as long as possible, even moving it from the back of her chair to the floor so it would be quieter. Tessa was enjoying dinner with Silas at Rio Italiana, the nicest restaurant in the hotel. She'd curled her hair and put on makeup that was actually visible without squinting. Gloria's guidance, of course. Her friend had even done her wings—so they were symmetrical for once.

She felt pretty, and they were having a nice time. Silas looked like a bronze statue. He was relaxed and telling funny stories. And Tessa felt relaxed too.

Except for that buzzing phone.

Finally, with an apologetic look at Silas, she leaned over and dug it out of her purse. "I should have left this thing at the hotel."

He waved a hand. "Go ahead and take it. Could be important."

Tessa glanced at the screen, which confirmed what she'd known in her gut. "It's definitely not important. It's my mother." She slid the bar on the screen. "Hi. I'm kinda busy. What's up?"

"Busy? Busy doing what? It's eight-thirty. You should be getting ready for bed. I already have my mask on."

Tessa rubbed her forehead, trying not to envision Cheryl with a bunch of green goo spread all over her face. "Mom! I'm at dinner. What's up?"

"Oh, nothing, really. I heard about poor Cynthia and wanted to see how the investigation is going."

Something in her tone made Tessa sit up straighter and pay closer attention. "I, uh, I don't really know. April's dealing with that. I haven't been questioned or anything. How'd *you* know about it?"

She remembered that Cheryl had known about Art's death too. There must be some kind of reaper grapevine that Tessa wasn't privy to yet. Maybe if she ever got a management position, she would be.

Briefly, Tessa wondered if the reaper grapevine worked by phone or email or something more archaic, like messenger bats or something. She knew the answer. The agency was so bureaucratic. It had to be email. But then there was Corwin Blade's message to her, something about a scythe? That was pretty arcane.

Of course, even if Cheryl knew what had happened through mystical means, Tessa couldn't question her too much about it at the moment. Silas sat two feet away from her, munching on a piece of garlic bread and having no idea his dining companion reaped the souls of the dead for a living.

She'd like to keep it that way as long as possible. Like, forever.

Cheryl spoke again, pulling Tessa out of her reverie with a vague answer. "Oh, I hear about things like this right away. So, do you have any idea what's going on? Are the souls lost? Or were they ever allocated?"

Tessa's eyes narrowed. "No. Why would I? I don't know what you mean."

"You were so good at finding Chet's soul, dear, that's all."

There was a pause on the line, during which Tessa's mind scrambled, trying to figure out Cheryl's endgame.

She got nowhere. Tessa had never been able to outsmart her mother. Her eyes flitted to Silas, who had finished the garlic bread and was digging into his pasta with the zeal of someone who'd spent all day in the sun and needed some calories.

She turned her body a bit, hoping to shield the mouthpiece so Silas would be less likely to hear Cheryl's voice wafting out. Tessa said, "Well, I don't believe April would exactly welcome my help."

"That may be. But if someone down there doesn't figure this out, I'll have to . . ." She trailed off, leaving only silence on the line again.

"You'll have to what?"

"Oh, nothing, dear. I was just thinking out loud. Go. Finish up dinner and get to bed. Your notes will suffer on less than eight hours of sleep. Nighty-night." Cheryl made a kiss-kiss noise and disconnected.

Silas glanced up from his spaghetti Bolognese. "Everything okay?"

"Well, my mom is nuts, but that's status quo. So, I guess everything's fine." She chuckled and tucked her purse away after silencing it. Then, she dove into the food in front of her.

The rest of the meal was pleasant, but only part of Tessa's attention was on the conversation. She kept thinking about her mom's half-sentence. What would Cheryl have to do if the mysteries of Art's and Cynthia's unaccounted-for deaths weren't solved?

After dinner, Silas and Tessa strolled slowly through the hotel.

"I'll walk you to your room," Silas offered.

"Okay, but let's take the elevator because I can't climb stairs with that tiramisu weighing me down."

"You got it." His hand found its way to the small of Tessa's back, giving her a little chill, as they headed for the lobby, where he punched the elevator button for her floor. "That was an excellent dessert, though. Worth not being able to climb stairs for." Silas rubbed his flat belly and radiated satisfaction.

"I have to agree with you there. Stairs are overrated anyway. Elevators are the way to go." She actually thought stairs may have been invented by the Grim Reaper. To kill people faster, by heart attack. Having met the man and felt his predatory gaze, she wouldn't put it past him.

She shook her head to clear out the image of the creepy Corwin Blade, drawing a questioning glance from Silas. Luckily, the elevator doors opened before he could question her.

Gloria and a few other reapers tumbled out into the lobby. They all wore pajamas. Gloria had on her hedgehog slippers. When she saw Tessa, she grabbed her elbow. "Emergency session," she said. "Come on."

Confusion clouded Silas' features. "You're having an emergency life insurance presentation at nine-thirty pm?"

Gloria shook her head. "This is about the agent who was killed by a shark, I think. They want to give us some information about her memorial. Or, you know, something. Sorry to steal Tessa away from you. Bye, now!" She pulled on Tessa's arm.

This was new. Usually, Gloria was shoving Tessa toward Silas, not trying to lead her away.

Over her shoulder, Tessa called, "Goodnight! I'll text you in the morning."

"Thanks for dinner!" Silas gave a little wave and headed for the door, still looking a bit baffled.

"What is this all about?" Tessa hissed, pulling her elbow out of Gloria's grip.

She shrugged. "I got a call that we needed to head to the main conference room for an emergency talk. You should've gotten one, too. That's all I know."

Tessa remembered her silenced phone. *Oops.*

As they filed into the conference room, Tessa caught a glimpse of April and Lee talking near where the buffet was set up in the morning. Lee's arms were crossed, and he frowned. April was talking earnestly to him.

It took about ten minutes for the room to fill with reapers. Some looked like they'd just come from the hotel bars, and they swayed slightly. Others were wearing pajamas and had mussed hair, as if they'd been sleeping already.

Finally, April moved behind the podium and tapped the microphone. "Okay, everyone. I'm sorry to have needed to call you down at this hour. But we thought it was important for you all to know that we've sorted out the circumstances surrounding the spate of unaccounted for deaths we've had recently." She paused, looking down as though consulting notes for a speech, even though the lectern was empty. No papers sat ready to help April know what to say.

The room was totally silent as everyone waited to hear the rest of the explanation. Or, as Tessa was thinking of it, for the other shoe to drop.

April pulled in a breath and looked up again. "It turns out, Cynthia was the problem all along. She failed to account for a few reaps in her home office. Then she missed reaping poor Art in the plane. And instead of admitting her mistakes or asking for help to fix the problem, we believe she simply made an allocation for herself to avoid coming clean."

The room filled with gasps and murmurs.

Tessa felt her face scrunch. Did April just say Cynthia chose to die by shark? To avoid getting into *work* trouble?

Cynthia *had* seemed pretty miserable, virtually from the first moment Tessa saw her. Maybe April was right?

But then Tessa thought about what Lee had said. That if there was an accounting error, it was Timothy who was the probable culprit. And Tessa had spoken to Cynthia herself about the problem. The other reaper had been adamant she hadn't messed up.

Tessa had believed her. She still did.

It was April who wasn't telling the truth. Tessa was sure of it.

But why? And if Cynthia hadn't allocated her own death, who had?

Chapter 13

The next morning, Tessa felt rejuvenated. A decent night's sleep and she'd only gorged herself on tiramisu, unlike the previous night with Gloria and room service.

As she showered, Tessa came up with a game plan for the day. She wasn't as convinced as April that Cynthia was responsible for the deaths—especially her own death. So, she was going to follow Timothy to the sessions he attended. Of course, she realized the potentially major flaw in her plan. Timothy's sessions were likely to be the ones April attended too.

And Tessa really didn't want to be stuck in a seat next to April. Like Cheryl, she'd probably expect Tessa to take notes.

Oh, well. Something fishy was going on, and Tessa had made up her mind to figure out what it was. Timothy was her biggest—well, her only—lead so far.

"Oof." Tessa surveyed the buffet table with a hand on her belly. "I can't do this to myself every day. I still haven't hit the gym."

Gloria wrinkled her nose. "You know, after last night, I've lost my appetite too. Coffee only."

"So, you aren't convinced either?"

"That Cynthia reaped herself?" Gloria raised a well-groomed eyebrow. "Of course not. I told your mother as much in an email earlier this morning."

"You did?"

"It's nothing. And don't worry. I told her you were a lovely roommate."

As they sipped coffee in the main conference room, Tessa kept an eye out for Timothy.

"What sessions are you going to attend today?" Gloria pushed her schedule sheet over so Tessa could see it.

Tessa shrugged. "I'm not sure." But she didn't look at the schedule—she found Timothy. He sat alone at a table and dug into a bowl of cereal. Within seconds, he'd splashed milk on his lapel and batted at it with a fistful of napkins.

"*How to Relax When the Reaping's Done* sounds good," Gloria mused. "I believe we already proved we have a handle on that with the company credit cart. How about *What to Talk About to Decrease Awkwardness on the Way to the Light.*"

"Mmm-hmm." Tessa had decided not to tell Gloria about her plan to follow Timothy. If she did, Gloria would probably either insist on joining Tessa, making it harder to be subtle about it, or try to talk her out of it, which she didn't have time for.

Timothy got up, put his bowl in a dish tub by the door, and headed out of the conference room.

Tessa shot to her feet. "I, uh, have to go to the bathroom before the first session. I'll catch you later. Save me a seat." She was gone before Gloria could utter a word.

In the hallway, she scanned every direction for Timothy's ill-fitting burgundy suitcoat. She just caught a glimpse of it as he rounded a corner. Tessa hurried that direction. But by the time she got around the corner herself, he was nowhere to be seen.

Wow. For such a clumsy guy, he actually has good shadow skills. He could give Bubba some tips.

Tessa rushed forward, glancing into each of the doorways as she passed through the hallway. But Timothy wasn't in any of them.

At an intersection with another hallway, she stopped and peeked around the corner. She looked left. There were quite a few reapers milling around there, but she couldn't spot tall, thin Timothy. When she turned to the right, a burgundy blur pushed through a doorway midway down the hall.

Tessa ran to catch up, thanking herself for not wearing heels that day. She leaned against the wall for a few minutes and counted slowly to forty before entering the room herself.

Timothy sat next to April in the front row. Tessa took a seat at the very back of the room.

The presenter, a reaper Tessa didn't know, had a sunny attitude and, if Tessa hadn't been focusing on Timothy so much, would have been fun to listen to. She was talking about how to get the most out of your day as a reaper—planning and scheduling your day so you could be given more assignments.

Tessa kept her eyes on Timothy. About fifteen minutes into the presentation, he looked at his watch, grabbed the notebook he'd been jotting in, and slipped out of the chair.

Tessa leaned over her own notebook, letting long hair fall forward to thwart Timothy's recognition. *Had he noticed her?* She counted slowly to twenty, grabbed her stuff, and darted after him.

He was nowhere to be seen. The hallway that was bustling earlier was now empty, as everyone was in their morning session.

Where is he? Had he gone back toward the hotel lobby? That made the most sense. The majority of the conference rooms where in that direction. Or maybe he'd wanted to go to two talks that were scheduled at the same time and decided to go halfsies.

She started in that direction but then hesitated and glanced the other way. The only thing there was a set of double doors that said Exit. One of them wasn't closed completely, as though someone had slipped out of it and not delivered enough momentum for the thing to swing back shut all the way.

Her brow furrowed. Why would Timothy leave the building? Did he need a smoke break or something? Tessa had never seen him with a cigarette, but she hadn't exactly been following him around everywhere before either. The guy, with his accountant-like aura, mostly blended in with the scenery.

Tessa opened the door cautiously and stuck her head outside. The sun was so bright she couldn't see anything for a minute. She blinked several times and held a hand to her forehead to shield her vision. Timothy was walking down a sidewalk that bordered the back of the hotel.

She eased out, holding the door until it closed so it wouldn't make noise. She dug in her purse for the sunglasses she'd bought with Silas, glad she had them with her even though she hadn't been planning to go outside that morning. Once they were on, her eyes were much more comfortable. She started after Timothy, making sure to stay far enough behind that it hopefully wouldn't trigger his sixth sense and let him know he was being followed.

At the end of the building, Timothy veered off across the perfectly manicured lawn, past a little courtyard with stone benches.

Where is he going?

Tessa tried to remember what Bubba had said during his talk about staying in the shadows. The main thing was to act normal. As much as possible, even forget yourself that you were following the person. That way, you wouldn't be putting out energy that may draw their attention.

She tried to think about something other than following Timothy across the lawn. First, her thoughts landed on Abi and Pepper. A smile lifted her lips as she remembered the need to pick up some gifts for Abi to make up for her cat's bad behavior. She should get Pepper a little something too. Poor kitty was probably just as irritated with Abi as the other way around.

The loud chirp of a bird startled her back to the moment. Her heart thudded faster as she remembered the mission. She scanned the landscape ahead for Timothy. He'd put more distance between them. The courtyard had given way to shorter, perfectly clipped grass.

In the distance, Tessa could see a few scattered golf carts.

Really? A golf course?

She couldn't believe it. Since becoming a reaper, Tessa had found herself on a golf course roughly triple the number of times she'd ever set foot on one during the whole rest of her life combined.

Was this some kind of curse? Were golf courses to reaper Tessa what graveyards were to most ordinary folk?

She rolled her eyes at her own thoughts and focused on Timothy. He'd stopped walking and stood, arms crossed, watching a group of golfers.

Tessa wanted to get as close as possible without being spotted by Timothy. There was a little creek to her left. She darted that direction and crouched in a patch of cattails, praying there were no alligators lurking there.

Then she stopped and blinked with the realization she wasn't the only reaper around. Lydia was there too. That was even more odd.

Lydia was approaching from a slightly different direction as Tessa and Timothy. The golfers waved her over and one of them requested a bag of chips and a soda, as though Lydia worked for the golf course. Tessa couldn't hear everything, but the scene was familiar. Her own first reap had been strikingly similar.

A moment later, one of the golfers stiffened and fell over. Tessa watched Lydia, in her grim reaper form, greet the man's spirit and herd him toward a bright light that only the two reapers could see.

But Timothy's gaze was right on them, above the other golfers. Could he see Lydia and the golfer's spirit too?

A shout went up from one of the other golfers, stopping the spirit momentarily, who looked down on his own prone body in the grass.

"I think he had a stroke or something! He's not breathing!"

The spirit looked sad. Lydia touched his arm, smiled, and drew his attention away from the ground and toward the sky.

Timothy nodded once, turned, and headed back across the course toward the hotel.

Tessa frowned. Why had Timothy taken it upon himself to watch Lydia reap a golfer? Why was Lydia even doing a reap here? Didn't Miami have its own office?

At least one thing was for sure—following Timothy had given Tessa more to chew on. Much more.

Chapter 14

Tessa stayed in the cattails until Lydia was done with the reap and heading back to the hotel. By then, the course had been swarmed by emergency and golf course personnel, and it was easy to blend in anyway.

Lydia went around to the front doors of the hotel. Tessa followed her inside. As soon as she set foot in the lobby, the scent of lunch wafted past Tessa's nose, making her stomach growl. Apparently, skipping breakfast meant something to her body and she needed more sustenance.

The hall outside the main conference room was loaded with food. Reapers teemed around it, piling their plates with sandwiches, veggies, and chips. Tessa thought it was weird how only the day prior it had been deserted when they'd called off the sessions after Cynthia's death. Today, it was like that had never happened. Business as usual—which only made sense because their business was death.

She didn't see Timothy anywhere, so Tessa kept one eye on Lydia as they both filled their plates. When she went into the conference room to eat, Tessa was glad to see Lydia sat alone at a round table at the edge of the room. She made a beeline to her. She smiled politely. "Hi! Care for some company?"

"Sure!" Lydia motioned to an empty chair. "Knock yourself out."

No sooner had Tessa settled in than Gloria appeared in the third chair at the table. She smiled brightly and then dug in.

"How are you doing, Lydia? You and Cynthia were friends, right?" Tessa took a bite of ham and cheese sandwich. At Lydia's nod, she said around it, "I'm so sorry for your loss."

"It was a shock. This whole conference has been full of *rotten* surprises." Lydia picked up a carrot stick but put it down again without taking a bite. "First Art, then Cynthia. I don't understand it."

"But April has all figured out." Tessa caught the sarcasm in Gloria's tone.

"You think?" Lydia tilted her head.

"Well, let's just say if she doesn't, I hope she figures it out soon." Gloria didn't say them out loud, but the words *before it happens again* hung in the air.

Tessa had been trying to figure out how to bring the conversation around to what she really wanted to know. She waited for a moment after Gloria spoke so the change in topic would be less abrupt and then said, "Lydia, what presentations did you attend this morning? It's so hard for me to choose which ones to go to and which ones to miss."

Lydia shrugged. "Actually, I worked this morning. Didn't go to any sessions."

Gloria's eyes snapped up at that. "Worked? You mean like you reaped someone?"

"Yeah. Timothy caught me before breakfast and told me to watch my reaper app. Said that life goes on and so does death. Or something sinister like that." She blew a breath up at a curl bouncing into her eye. "It was a golfer having a stroke, which is kinda funny in a very morbid way. Timothy said that, because it was happening on the hotel's golf course property, it made the most sense to assign a reaper from the conference to it." She picked up a cherry tomato, examined it, and set it down again. "It was nice to get some fresh air, I guess."

"Oh, yeah, that makes sense." Gloria attacked her food with renewed zeal, satisfied with Lydia's answer.

Lydia stood. "I guess I don't have much of an appetite. I'm going to head to my room for a nap before afternoon sessions. See you gals later."

Tessa watched the other reaper leave the room and then leaned over to Gloria. "That's not the full scoop. Timothy followed Lydia to her assignment this morning. Stood there and watched her. It was like he could see the whole thing."

"Oh, yeah. I'm pretty sure people in his position are given the gift of Sight. In case they need to do an audit or something. Sounds like that's what he was doing with Lydia." Gloria seemed nonplussed. She frowned at her empty plate. "I'm still hungry."

Tessa still wasn't satisfied. "But why would Timothy follow her today? During the conference. He left in the middle of a session to follow Lydia."

Gloria glanced at Tessa. "And how, exactly, do you know that?"

She looked at her plate and mumbled, "Because I followed *him*."

"Ah." Gloria chuckled. "Well, maybe he wanted to make sure Lydia is doing things by the book. He's April's lackey, after all. Maybe they're worried that, after Cynthia's death, she'd failed to perform her duties."

Tessa wasn't so sure that was the reason. "I'm going to ask Timothy about it," she decided.

"Okay. Have fun with that. I'm going to get some more food."

Gloria hadn't been gone for a minute when Lee Stuart lowered himself into her chair. He smiled and gestured at her almost empty plate. "Nice lunch today, eh?"

"I guess. It hit the spot."

He rubbed his abdomen. "Sure did. Hey, listen, I was sitting over there," he gestured to a nearby table, "eating by myself and preparing for my talk. I saw you over here, and I thought you should come. It's right up your alley. It's called *Advancements in Your Reaper Career: How to Make it to Upper Management.*"

She was only in her first year as a reaper. Tessa didn't want to think about advancing yet. She must have given him a look that said as much because Lee waved a hand. "Anyway, I also couldn't help but overhear you say you plan to talk to Timothy about following that reaper on an assignment. I wanted to warn you—he's a pretty squirrelly guy. Whatever you do, don't go talk to him alone."

She tipped her head a bit, considering him. Timothy was taller than Tessa but seemed like he had no substance at all. She felt like she could push him over easily if he tried anything.

"I'm here to be your wingman if you need one," Lee offered.

"Thanks. I'll keep it in mind." She got up and grabbed her plate. "See you later." As she left the room, Tessa scanned it for Timothy. There was no sign of him.

She bussed her plate and went into the outer room. There were still a few reapers hanging around the buffet table, but it was slim pickings now. It was as though a flock of hungry vultures has descended on it. Only some sad-looking salami and a few wilted pieces of celery remained.

Tessa didn't see Timothy there either. Talking to him about Lydia would have to wait.

She pulled out the presentation schedule from her purse and scanned it. There was slim pickings there too. Three of the sessions were repeats of talks she'd already been to. One was about how to sell actual life insurance if you had to. The only remaining one was Lee's talk on advancement.

With a sigh, Tessa stuffed the paper back in her purse and headed toward the room Lee's talk was supposed to be in.

As she went, she thought about Lydia's reap and why Timothy had been there. Was Gloria right that he was simply acting as April's stooge—micromanaging the help for his irritable boss?

It didn't quite ring true to Tessa. Neither did Timothy's explanation about the reap itself. There must be an agency in Miami, and not everyone there would be attending the conference. Why weren't they given the allotment instead of Lydia?

She stumbled to a halt when someone stepped in front of her, blocking the way into the conference room. All she saw was a burgundy suit. Tessa's head jerked up.

It was Timothy.

"Have you been following me?"

Chapter 15

Timothy's expression was deadpan. Tessa swallowed hard. Her mind raced as she tried to figure out what to say.

Suddenly, he laughed and clapped her on the arm. "Just joshing you. Seems like I keep seeing you everywhere. But it's a conference. I guess we're all basically in the same area most of the time."

Her laugh came out more nervous than she wanted it to, so Tessa cut it short. She straightened her shoulders. "You know, speaking of following, why did you follow Lydia this morning?"

Timothy's eyebrows rose in a question.

Okay, she'd blurted that right out. Now she had to stick to her guns. "Sorry. I needed some air. That presentation was kind of boring. I happened to see you crossing the courtyard and wandered that direction myself. I didn't realize there was a golf course over there. Then I saw Lydia doing a reap and you watching her."

He blew out a breath and looked at his feet. "Here's the thing." His eyes darted to both sides as though checking for eavesdroppers. "I have aspirations of becoming a reaper. At least, I did—until seeing what happened to Cynthia." He paused, and a shudder wracked his thin frame. "It made me think I must not be cut out for it after all."

Tessa could understand that. She was already a reaper, and most every reap made her re-evaluate her career choice. Cynthia's death had doubled down on that feeling for a hot second.

Timothy averted his gaze. "So, I arranged for one of our reapers to get an allocation this morning and followed her to watch. I wanted to prove to myself I could still be a reaper if I wanted to." He finally met Tessa's gaze again. She couldn't tell what the emotion was that played there.

"And did you? Prove it to yourself, I mean?"

His thin shoulders rose and fell. "I'm not sure." He cleared his throat. "But the Miami office appreciated our help this morning. A lot of their folks are here at the conference, too, and their remaining reapers have been stretched pretty thin. I told them to just let me know if they need us to take any allocations off their hands."

"That was nice of you."

"Would you still think so if I send the next assignment to you?"

She pursed her lips and studied him.

Timothy waved a hand. "I promise I won't follow you. I got the information I needed from Lydia's reap. I just have to do some soul-searching on my own now."

"Fine," Tessa agreed.

"Thank you." He stepped aside and swept a hand toward the conference room. "Enjoy your session." As he walked away, he said over his shoulder, "Don't forget to watch your app."

Tessa found a seat at the back of the conference room, pulled out her phone, and made sure it would vibrate if the reaper app went off during the presentation. Lee gave her a smile and a wave as he entered the room and headed for the lectern.

Her mind wandered during the talk. She thought about Timothy wanting to be a reaper. Was that strictly an up-and-up aspiration? Or could the guy have more evil intentions? Like, was it possible he was a serial killer wanting to use reaping to do it? Maybe he'd been unable to secure a reaper job, so he'd had to use his accounting chops to do some killing.

Tessa remembered the lack of blood perfusion in Timothy's face after seeing Cynthia and dismissed that potential theory. The guy was almost certainly not a serial killer.

But perhaps his desire to be a reaper meant Timothy wasn't appropriately allocating deaths for another selfish reason. Could he have put in the order for Art's death hoping to talk April into giving Timothy the empty position? And then, when that didn't happen, arranged for Cynthia's death for another shot at a job?

It made sense. More than the serial killer thing. It qualified as a motive.

Tessa's phone lit up, and she grabbed it, half-expecting to see an assignment on the reaper app. But was it safe to go on a reap ordered by Timothy? Was it truly official or was his explanation a lie? He seemed to be onto the fact that Tessa was following him. Would he order her death next, in an attempt to get her job?

But it wasn't the reaper app that had caused the notification. It was a missed call from Cheryl. Tessa put the phone down and made a mental note to check for a voicemail from her mother later.

At the end of the day's presentations, Tessa checked her phone again. There was no message from Cheryl, but as she looked at the screen, a text from Silas appeared. It was as though he'd been watching for the clock to strike five and Tessa to be done for the day.

Dinner date? I've got a hankerin' for Thai.

Tessa blinked at the word *date* but then shook her head. It was just a figure of speech. If she wanted to hone in on a word in the text to obsess over, it should be hankerin'. Who said that? And actually spelled it with an apostrophe in a text? Maybe Silas was the sociopath.

Chuckling to herself, Tessa tapped the reaper app to check it once more.

Nothing.

She went to text him back but stopped midway. She chewed her bottom lip for a second.

Silas texted again: *Does this mean you don't want Thai? I could go for Indian instead. BBQ? Empanadas again? I'm easy.*

Laughing, she decided Timothy must have decided to give the next assignment to someone else. Or maybe the local agency hadn't shifted one over to him after all. She texted back: *Mediterranean? Polynesian? A dinner date sounds great.*

She held her breath, wishing after hitting send that there was some way to get the text back and change the word *date*. Sure, Silas had used it first, but it could have been a figure of speech. She didn't have to use it too, shining a huge figurative spotlight on it.

His return text was perfectly normal, belying her obsession over the little word: *Pick you up in 15.*

Tessa went to her room, changed into a light blue sundress, and sent a text to Gloria: *Going out with Silas.*

The return text came back lightning fast: *See you later. Remember: be spontaneous Tessa.*

Tessa rolled her eyes as she left the hotel room, slipping the phone into her purse after unmuting the notifications.

Silas had just entered the lobby when Tessa got out of the elevator. He beamed at her. "How was your day?"

"Fine. How about you? How's that jellyfish sting?"

His already bronze cheeks darkened even more. "Fine. Much better now. That isn't something I want to experience again, though. Ready to head out?" He grabbed her elbow.

With a nod, Tessa let him lead her out into the clear evening.

In the end, they decided on Thai after all. Silas had already scoped out a place near the boardwalk.

"I sat on the beach near here for a while at lunchtime, and the place was crazy busy," he explained. "I figured they must have decent food." He grinned as they settled into their chairs. "How about some appetizers?"

"Yes. I'm starved."

Her phone buzzed.

Tessa winced as she had a premonition about what that buzz meant. With reluctance, she pulled the phone out of her purse to confirmed it. Yep. It was the reaper app.

She had an assignment. And it was nearby—at the pier.

Tessa glanced at Silas. "Um. Can you order for us while I run out for a few minutes?"

"Where do you need to go?" He rose halfway from the chair. "I'll just go with you. We can come back afterward."

She shook her head and reached over to push him back into the chair. "No, no. I just have to meet Gloria and give her my pass key to the room. She lost hers."

He sank down. "Oh, well, that's easy. She can just get a new one at the hotel's front desk. I had to do it a couple days ago."

"She doesn't have any ID on her to prove who she is. It's all inside the room. It'll just take me a few minutes. Why don't you order a few appetizers for us? I'll be right back." With a reassuring smile, Tessa hurried off, hoping he'd bought her excuse.

She paused outside the restaurant to check her reaper app. When she saw who the deceased was, Tessa frowned, and her stomach flopped. Grudgingly, she tapped the assignment to accept it, and a map popped up with Tessa's position marked by a glowing green dot and the assignment's in yellow. The reap was surrounded by blue water, all the way at the end of the pier.

Tessa hurried in that direction, hoping she could get done quickly and back to Silas before the appetizers got cold.

When she arrived, Tessa scanned the area, looking for the person that matched the picture in her app. She found her right away.

A mother stood by the railing, looking out at the ocean. She held the hand of a little girl who looked to be about two or three and moved a stroller slowly back and forth with the other.

Tessa's heart squeezed. She started forward but then a thought skittered across her mind.

Is this right?

It didn't feel right. Of course, Tessa knew bad things happened sometimes, but right here, right now, things just felt . . . off.

Why was Timothy allocating deaths to conference-going reapers? Was his explanation about helping the Miami agency true? Or was something else going on?

Could he be manipulating the allocations to get the numbers right after Cynthia's unauthorized death?

Tessa made a snap decision. She moved forward quickly, toward the young family. When the mother let go of the little girl's hand and turned to lift the baby out of the stroller, Tessa broke into a run.

She made it there just in a time. There was a spot of railing, under construction, where the only thing holding anyone back was some caution tape and a cone. As the girl began to wobble on the edge, about to fall into the choppy waters where she was scheduled to die, Tessa grabbed her under the arms, pulling her gently back.

The mother snatched up the girl's hand. "Oh my goodness! I can't believe that almost happened. I was getting Davey out of his stroller. Dani, you can't go near the edge! Look! There's no rail!" Her voice was gentle but held the barely restrained panic of someone who understood what had almost happened. She looked at Tessa. "Thank you so much. How did you . . ."

"I was in the right place at the right time, that's all. I happened to see your little girl get close to the edge." Tessa smiled at the woman.

"Thank you. I've been . . . having a hard time lately. Since my husband left. I just wanted us to come out and see the ocean. You know, relax for a minute." She shook her head. "I should have known better. My kiddos are still so young." She blinked back tears.

Tessa shook her head. "It was just one of those things. Kids are so fast." Tessa walked with them, grabbing the stroller and pushing while the woman carried Davey and held tightly to Dani's hand. "I'm sorry to hear about your husband."

The woman nodded. "It's probably for the best." She glanced at Dani. It was clear she didn't want to say too much in front of the girl about her father.

"I've had my share of rotten relationships." Tessa thought about Frank, her most recent ex-boyfriend. He had been a real jerk. "But I still think there are good guys out there." An image of Silas danced in her mind's eye, making her smile.

The young mother smiled too. "I know. I just have to focus on my kiddos for right now." She didn't let go of Dani's hand but leaned forward. "Thanks again. I . . . I think you saved her life."

Tessa nodded, gave Dani one last smile, and headed down the boardwalk toward the Thai restaurant. But after only a couple of steps, Silas stepped out of the shadows in front of her.

His face was covered with confusion. "Where's Gloria?" He glanced at Dani and her mother. "And what just happened? How did you know that girl was going to fall in the water? Did your phone tell you that?"

Tessa arranged her face into an innocent expression. "What?" She glanced over her shoulder at the trio she'd just left. "Oh. Um. No. It didn't. I just happened to be walking by and saw her wobbling on the edge."

He shook his head. "That was . . . awesome how you saved her. But I swear it wasn't random. You came directly here. Walked right out there and grabbed that girl. As though you knew it was about to happen." His brow furrowed. "How is that possible?"

"It's not. Gloria told me to meet her here. But she found her key. Why did you follow me?"

He shrugged. "It's just this feeling I have. Since back home in Mist River. Remember the casino thing?" He stepped closer. "Tessa, I really like you. Like, enough that I want to be in a relationship with you."

Her heart beat faster.

"But something isn't quite right. There's something going on with you." He crossed his arms. "Can't you just tell me what it is so we can move on? So I can feel like you aren't lying to me?"

She pressed her lips together, considering. Gloria had suggested that it may be okay for Silas to know the truth at some point. But now certainly wasn't the time. He'd only just mentioned the word relationship. It had to be much further down the road.

But she couldn't be upset with him for following her. If he was the one acting weird all the time, she'd probably try to investigate too. No, she definitely would.

Except she couldn't tell Silas the truth about her job. Not yet.

She smiled. "Silas, there's nothing going on. I swear. Like I said, Gloria texted me that she found her pass key. I happened to look out and see that lady with the girl and a stroller. I had one of those feeling—you know, a hunch. Something made me start walking toward them and then I saw Dani wobbling and ran to grab her. That's the girl's name—Dani." Tessa shrugged it off as no big deal. "My stomach is growling. Do we still have our table at the Thai place?"

Silas still looked a little suspicious, but his expression softened slightly. "Yes. I left my credit card as collateral. We should have a big tray of hot spring rolls waiting for us." He held out an elbow. "Let's go."

She breathed a sigh of relief as the energy between them seemed to settle back to normal.

But, at the same time, her stomach dropped. That had been a close one. Silas was too smart for Tessa to keep her secret from him for long.

She'd been stupid to think they may be able to have a romantic relationship.

Chapter 16

They had a pleasant dinner, even though the heavy feeling never really left Tessa's stomach. She and Silas went on a short walk on the beach after the Thai food, and then he dropped her off at the hotel.

The weight of the untruth between them still held something back for him too. There was no almost kiss. No grazing of hands. Tessa had put so much thought behind the word date from his text, only to ruin it by being a reaper.

She went straight up the room, not expecting Gloria to be there, since it wasn't even nine o'clock yet. The crowd at the bar partied until at least midnight.

But as she pushed the door open, the toes on a pair of socked feet wiggled at the end of Gloria's bed.

"Oh . . . I didn't expect you to be here." She'd actually wanted some alone time. Tessa pushed open the door the rest of the way.

"That's because you never answer your phone, dear." Cheryl sat on Gloria's bed, back against the headboard, flipping through a home decorating magazine.

The door swung shut behind her. Frantic, Tessa's eyes swept the room. This felt like a surreal dream. Gloria's gold suitcase was gone from the luggage rack, replaced by a navy-blue one. In fact, all of Gloria's stuff had vanished.

"Mom. What are you doing here? And what did you do with Gloria?"

Cheryl flipped another page and kept her eyes on the magazine. "The problems here are too grand. We can't allow the conference to continue without our intervention. The task force was called up this morning."

Tessa dropped her phone and pass key on the dresser. "Task force? What . . . wait. You're a member of the super-secret task force that comes in to handle things when a soul is lost or whatever?"

Cheryl raised a perfectly shaped eyebrow. "Not *a member*, Theresa. I'm *the head* of the task force."

Tessa sank onto her own bed and ran a hand through her hair. It had gotten knotted up a bit during her walk with Silas on the windy beach. She felt off-kilter. Her mind was sluggish as she tried to catch up with what was happening. "You didn't answer my question. Where's Gloria?"

Tessa's heart fluttered as, momentarily, she wondered if her friend was okay—if maybe her actions had triggered Timothy into offing another reaper. But Cheryl had said this morning. Nothing had happened this morning.

"We moved her to a single room. I thought it would be nice to bunk with my daughter." She finally looked over at Tessa. "Like old times."

Tessa pressed her lips together. There was something odd in her mother's expression . . . the hint of an emotion she couldn't remember seeing there before. If she didn't know better, Tessa would have said it was vulnerability.

She nodded. "That sounds like fun, Mom." She managed not to choke on the word *fun*. "But wait. If you're the head of the task force, why did you make me find Chet Sanborn's spirit by myself?"

The strangely vulnerable expression on Chery's face disappeared, replaced by amusement. She waved a hand. "Oh, that. I didn't want to get involved unless it was required. And look! You did just fine."

Tessa narrowed her eyes, thinking about the stress she'd gone through during her first week on the job. Her mother could have helped relieve that and decided not to?

Cheryl licked her finger to pry open the next page. "Oh, please. Don't get your knickers in a knot. I was paying attention. I could have jumped in to help any time. But I thought it was a valuable learning experience. And I was right. You've jumped into your career with more knowledge than most at this stage. You *should* be thanking me."

"No. You told me there was going to be an apocalypse if I didn't find Mr. Sanborn." Tessa's tone was accusatory.

Cheryl chuckled. "Well, I may have exaggerated a touch. But, really, it is true that things can go awry fast with the fabric of the universe if the accounting is off for too long." She set the magazine aside and swung her legs over the bed, facing Tessa. "Tell me. What have you dug up on this current situation?"

Tessa didn't want to change subjects. She still felt pouty about the revelation that Cheryl was on the task force. But she knew from years of experience that once Cheryl had decided that a topic of discussion was over, she wasn't likely to entertain it further. "Not a whole lot."

"Really? Gloria says you've been snooping."

Traitor!

"Timothy . . . April's assistant . . . he's my biggest suspect right now."

"Timothy?" Cheryl cocked her head as though it would help her access data in her brain about the man. "Timothy.

That man from the office last week. He's awfully mousey, isn't he?"

Tessa shrugged. "I guess so. He wants to be a reaper. I think maybe he's killing reapers to make a job opening for himself."

"A little extreme, isn't it? What brought you to this conclusion?"

"It's not a conclusion. Not yet. But I don't really have any other leads." She flopped back onto the bed and talked to the ceiling instead of Cheryl. "Lee Stuart told me that, if there was an allocation issue in the eastern district, it was Timothy who'd be behind it. He seemed to think Timothy was easily distracted by nonsense and could have messed up the accounting on accident."

"And you agree?"

"I'm not sure. I mean, Timothy has been on the outskirts of all the weird things going on. He was on the plane when Art died and nearby when Cynthia was attacked by a shark. And he's doling out allocations here."

"Here? In Miami?"

"Yes." Tessa nodded. "There have been two reaps that I know of so far. He sent Lydia on one—a stroke on the golf course. And he followed her to watch. Mom, he told me he did that to see if he still had the chops to be a reaper after he got squeamish during Cynthia's death. Then, he assigned a reap to me."

"You?" Cheryl's tone was sharp, tinged with alarm.

Tessa got onto one elbow to look at her mother. "Yep. I was supposed to reap a little girl. A drowning. But I didn't do it."

"You lost the soul?"

"No. I saved the little girl."

Cheryl's eyes got wide. "You what?" Her words were barely above a whisper.

Tessa shook her head and sat up all the way. "Something didn't feel right. I think Timothy was messing with the numbers. Like, he allocated the little girl's death to make the numbers add up or something." She leaned forward. "I just had this strong gut feeling that she wasn't supposed to die." She shrugged. "So, I saved her."

Cheryl blew out a breath. "Okay. I don't know if I can get you out of this one, Theresa. If you saved a soul that was truly supposed to cross over . . . well, that's very, very bad."

For the first time since she'd yanked Dani back onto the pier, Tessa felt a ripple of doubt. "Like what?"

"Like you could be court-martialed and sentenced to life in federal prison." In answer to the questioning look Tessa shot her, she explained, "We contract out to them in these situations. A few people high up in the government know about us." She stood and began to pace. "But that isn't important now. What's important is proving Timothy is the culprit and that he ordered a death, or more than one, that shouldn't have occurred. We need to be proactive about defending you."

Tessa twisted her fingers together. "How, exactly, do we do that?"

Cheryl grabbed her pass key and purse and spun toward the door. "*We* don't do anything. *You* go to bed and stay out of trouble. I'm going to consult with the rest of the task force."

She was gone before Tessa could say anything else.

Tessa was left staring at the back of the door, wondering what else her mom kept secret from her.

***

The next morning when Tessa woke up, Cheryl wasn't there. It was clear she'd been back and left again because the clothes she'd been wearing the night before were on her bed and a damp used towel lay on the bathroom floor.

Tessa was obviously still catching up on sleep from the late night out with Silas at the beginning of the convention. It felt like another time. Another her.

She took her time getting ready, Cheryl's warning about a court martial and federal prison dominating her troubled thoughts.

When Tessa finally managed to push away that worry, another one popped up—Silas. Had she made a mistake spending so much time with him? He was clearly getting the feeling that Tessa was keeping something from him. If they continued their relationship, that could increase. He could get hurt.

But maybe it would be okay once that got back to Mist River and weren't surrounded by reapers—and a rogue administrator ordering bogus reaps.

Tessa hadn't come to any conclusions by the time she was dressed. With a sigh, she grabbed her purse and headed out and immediately spotted Gloria, who was coming out of a room across the hall.

Gloria grinned. "Nice surprise last night, huh?"

"If by nice, you mean terrifying and annoying, then yes. Having my mother slash boss show up in my room unannounced was *nice*." Tessa rolled her eyes.

"She said she called to tell you to expect her. You didn't answer or call back."

"She's never heard of voicemail," Tessa shot back. "Seriously, if what she had to say was important, she'd leave a message or text it to me."

Gloria punched the down button on the elevator. "I guess you deserved the surprise, then. What's she here for, anyway? Did she decide at the last minute that she wanted to get her learnin' on? Or is she presenting? Seems weird, since this is the last day of the conference."

They got into the empty elevator. "She's the head of the task force that investigates lost souls and such," Tessa explained. "She's here to help handle the deaths of Art and Cynthia."

Gloria whistled. "Wow. I don't think you're supposed to say things like that out loud," she whispered, "the mythical task force is real. And Cheryl's the head of it. That's how you say it."

They exited the elevator into the lobby, where reapers milled about or huddled in groups of two and three, talking in hushed tones. Tessa had a feeling that word of Cheryl's arrival and what it meant had gotten out.

The breakfast buffet was crowded too. April was scheduled to give her wrap-up speech in the big conference room while people ate. Gloria and Tessa carried their plates and cups of coffee in and stood for a minute, looking for spots to sit. There weren't many left, and they ended up in the front row, next to Bubba, who was beside Lee.

And to Lee's other shoulder, Cheryl sat sipping coffee and looking calm. She glanced at her daughter, her gaze dropping to Tessa's plate. She pressed her lips together, and Tessa knew her mother was judging her breakfast choices. Tessa lifted her chin, set the plate down, and took a big bite of donut in defiance.

April made her way to the podium and tapped the microphone. She looked paler than usual, and her eyes lingered on Cheryl for a second before darting away. She began to speak, talking about how well the conference had gone—considering—and how much knowledge had been passed back and forth between reapers.

Tessa nibbled and listened with half an ear. April's tone was flat, her words more halting than usual. But she wasn't saying anything particularly interesting, and Tessa preferred people-watching.

After ten minutes of droning on, April seemed to be wrapping up. "Our profession is an old and venerated one. As reapers, we are chosen for a sacred job. Gathering like this to help one another learn to do that job to the best of our abilities is an essential part of maintaining the integrity of our careers. I salute you all for attending and wish you luck over the next year. Until we meet again."

April turned away from the microphone, toward Timothy, who approached his boss with a file.

Cheryl stood and cleared her throat, causing the murmur of voices that had begun to rise in the room to decrease back to silence again.

Lee and Bubba got to their feet too, and the three reapers edged out of the row of chairs and approached April and Timothy.

Tessa perked up. Lee and Bubba were on the task force?

Cheryl spoke in a clear, ringing voice that seemed enhanced somehow, as though she wore an invisible microphone. "Yes, we do have a sacred mandate to help the dead cross over. We also have a responsibility to police ourselves—to ensure that those who are within the fold of our organization have impeccable ethics. Unfortunately, we have reason to believe there's been a problem. The Task Force on Lost Souls and Misplaced Allocations," she glanced at Lee and Bubba, "has found reasonable proof that Timothy Bond has engaged in unlawful activities resulting in the deaths of reapers and the misallocations of their souls."

Bubba stepped forward, reaching for Timothy, whose face drained. He looked even paler than on the dock at the time of Cynthia's death. His hands began to shake. He dropped the file.

"But . . . but I didn't do anything," Timothy objected.

Bubba made a strange motion with his hands and a pair of handcuffs appeared in them. But they weren't standard-issue police variety cuffs. They looked like they were made of silver electricity, and they sparkled and snapped as Bubba grabbed Timothy's left wrist.

"Of course, you'll be able to present your defense to the judge," Cheryl said, not unkindly. "If you have a lawyer, you can call them once we get you to a secure location. If you don't, one will be appointed for you."

Bubba pushed one end of the magical cuffs against Timothy's skin, and the loop went right through his wrist, then clamped down. With a swift motion, Bubba grabbed Timothy's right wrist and repeated the motion with the other end of the cuffs. Once they were on, the handcuffs disappeared from view. Timothy was able to hold his hands at his sides. Tessa realized the task force would be able to remove Timothy from the premises without any non-reapers who may be around realizing he was restrained.

Timothy turned toward April. His tone was desperate. "Tell them I didn't do it! I'm a good employee. An honest one."

April rubbed her temple and blew out a breath. "This is the most ridiculous thing I've seen in my career," she snapped. "Timothy is nothing but an assistant. If you take him, how am I going to get everything done? I don't even know how to run the data base."

Cheryl crossed her arms. "We'll assign you a temporary assistant until this is sorted out.

April opened her mouth to say something else but then shrugged and addressed Timothy. "There's nothing I can do. The task force, on official business, outranks me. You'll just have to go with them. My hands are tied."

Timothy's chin dropped to his chest. "But I'm not guilty."

"Let's go." Bubba grabbed Timothy's elbow and propelled him forward.

Lee turned toward the room at large and gave a relaxed smile. "As you can see, we have this under control. Please relax and enjoy the last day of the conference."

The task force left with Timothy, who whimpered and cast looks of panic back at April. She ignored him, carefully gathering the papers form the podium as though that were the most important thing she'd do all day.

Once the task force and Timothy were gone, the room erupted in excited chatter.

Gloria said, "Well, that was fast. I guess that's why the task force gets the big bucks. Can you believe Bubba's on it?" She looked amused.

"No!" But Tessa was only partly listening to Gloria. Her mind was on what had just happened.

She'd nearly been convinced that Timothy was behind the recent reaper deaths and extra Miami allocations. But not completely. There had still been a whisper of doubt. When she'd talked to Timothy, he'd seemed genuine. Still, the order for Dani's death hadn't felt right to Tessa. And Timothy must have been behind that.

Yes, he must be the culprit.

Still, as she bussed her dishes and left the conference room, Tessa had a strange, worried feeling in the pit of her stomach.

What if they had the wrong guy?

Chapter 17

Tessa excused herself from the table at lunch and returned to her room to rest a little and freshen up—which meant take a quick nap and hope it didn't rearrange her hair into a hopeless rats' nest before the evening's activities.

But Cheryl was already there, using the mirror above one of the dressers to reapply lipstick. She glanced at her daughter. "Oh, good. I was afraid you wouldn't bother to pack until after I'm trying to sleep tonight. Glad to see you'll be getting it done now."

Tessa knew that was a Cheryl code of instruction—a maneuver to get her way without demanding it.

Tessa sighed. She hadn't any intention to pack yet. In fact, her plan pretty much *had* been to do it after the awards dinner that would mark the end of the conference that night. After all, they weren't flying out until late the next morning. There was no sense in wasting time she could spend napping or lying by the pool this afternoon.

But she didn't feel like arguing with her mother, so she opened her carry-on and started re-organizing what had become a rumpled mess of clothes. While doing so, Cheryl bobbed in and out of her periphery. "So, that was exciting this morning—the task force arresting Timothy. How did you decide he was behind the unallocated deaths?"

Cheryl popped the top on her lipstick tube and turned away from the mirror. "Oh, you know. Investigative skills—blah, blah. Nothing too exciting, dear."

Tessa pursed her lips for a second and then blew out a breath. "Okay. As long as you didn't arrest him based on what I said last night . . ."

"Hmm?" Cheryl was rummaging in her suitcase, and she cast a glance over her shoulder at Tessa. "Of course not. We did our own thorough examination of the records and interviewed people here at the conference."

"Did you interview April?" Tessa wondered. Ever since Timothy had been taken away in magical handcuffs, Tessa hadn't been able to concentrate on the conference. Her thoughts had been wrapped up in the murder investigation. Well, the same could be said about the whole conference—since Art's death.

It still seemed like a mystery. And she couldn't shrug off the idea that they'd gotten the wrong man. In fact, her suspicions had shifted toward April. The woman wasn't very nice. In some ways, she reminded Tessa of Cheryl.

And April had an ongoing competition with Lee Stuart. Maybe she'd been the one to mess with the allocations. Or perhaps she'd strong-armed Timothy into doing it. That actually made more sense, since Timothy was the brains of the operation—or at least of the accounting. April had said it herself, she couldn't even log into the system. And with the way April treated him, it was unlikely he'd be able to resist her orders.

A new thought occurred to Tessa. Maybe that was why Timothy had looked so pale on the dock when Cynthia was killed. Perhaps he'd felt guilty for following April's orders.

Cheryl hummed as she buzzed around the room picking things up to pack. She'd only been there one night. Yet, she'd unpacked and now repacked like she was there for the week.

Tessa eyed her, wondering how to approach the subject. Finally, she cleared her throat. "What will happen to Timothy now? Federal court martial?"

"Oh, he'll get a fair trial." Cheryl's tone was vague. "But it will be Mr. Blade who ultimately decides what to do with him."

Mr. Blade! Of course.

"When will that happen? And where?" Tessa bit her lip. Maybe she could speak to Mr. Blade in time. "Will it be here in Miami?"

Cheryl shrugged. "That's not my area. The task force will hold Timothy safely until we receive further instructions."

"Hold him? Hold him where?"

Cheryl's eyebrows rose a fraction. "What are you up to, Theresa?" She crossed to pick up her phone from the nightstand.

Tessa held up her hands placatingly. "Nothing. Why would you think I'm up to something? I'm just curious. Is Timothy in some kind of government facility? Miami jail? Reaper prison? Inquiring minds want to know these things."

Cheryl sat on the edge of the bed, scrolling on her phone. She seemed distracted. "He's here in the hotel. You know that group from Albuquerque with the stomach bug left early, so the sixth floor is mostly empty. We secured a room there. The task force members are taking turns guarding him until someone from the main office comes and gets him. They're traveling here from D.C."

"Ah. Well, I'm glad that's over with." Tessa pulled out a swimsuit and closed her suitcase. "I think I'll go hang out at the pool one last time."

Cheryl's attention was still on her phone. "Have fun, dear."

Tessa changed, slipping a cover-up over her suit, and got out of there fast, before her mother's distraction ended and she re-focused on her daughter.

As Tessa headed toward the pool, she kept her eyes peeled for Mr. Blade. She remembered how Silas hadn't seemed to see Blade before. Was that because Silas wasn't a reaper?

But no. When Tessa first met Blade in the hallway outside the conference room, other reapers had scattered out of his way but hadn't looked directly at him. It was as though they'd sensed his presence in a way but couldn't actually see him.

Tessa thought it was possible—maybe even likely—that Corwin Blade was only visible to people when he wanted to be. So, looking for him could be entirely a waste of time. If he didn't want Tessa to find him, she may walk right past without even knowing he was there.

Still, she scanned the area for his tall, dark frame. At the pool, she pulled out her purple sunglasses, popped them on, and looked around.

No Corwin Blade, aka the Grim Reaper himself.

She found a chair and sat, not leaning back, and tried to put out vibes that she wanted to talk to Blade. Maybe she could will him to appear? Or maybe he could feel when a reaper reached out for him?

That reminded her of what he'd told her. Something about the Scythe.

But surely, Blade could just sort of . . . know . . . whether Timothy was telling the truth about the allocations? After all, he was the original version, right? Every reaper was doing a tiny bit of what was really, ultimately, Blade's job. They'd been given some of his abilities, somehow. So, Blade would know whether the numbers were messed up and who was responsible.

Tessa sat for an hour, mulling over the situation and watching for Mr. Blade, who never arrived.

When her phone buzzed, she pulled it out with a sigh, resigned that he wasn't going to show up just because she'd tried to summon him.

Silas had texted: *One last vacation sunset. Want to come?*

A smile leapt to her lips, and she texted back *Yes* without really giving it much thought.

But I have to change.

Cool. I'll pick you up in 20 minutes.

Tessa was glad to find her hotel room empty. Cheryl must have gone downstairs. Or maybe she was taking her turn guarding Timothy. Wherever she was, Tessa was happy to change her clothes in peace and leave without having to explain to her mother where she was going.

Silas was right on time, as usual, and he gave her a warm, tight hug. Tessa relaxed in his arms.

Should she be doing this? Was it unfair to Silas to hang out with him when she was pretty sure they'd need to put an end to the budding relationship? He seemed to be over the weirdness of the night before—the lie that she'd told him.

She pushed away the doubts that tried to niggle their way between her and Silas. She was determined to live in the moment as much as possible for one more evening.

"Last chance to visit the empanada truck," Silas suggested as they went outside.

She shook her head. "Sounds amazing, but we have our awards dinner tonight. Gloria said they really do it up with some great food." She patted her stomach. "I'd better save my calories."

Silas chuckled and grabbed her hand as they got to the boardwalk. "Well, if I have to have you back at a certain time, I'd better take advantage of every minute." He glanced at her. "You know, I've had a great time hanging out with you."

"Yeah." She returned his smile and squeezed his hand. "Me too. It's been a blast."

"Thanks for suggesting it. And talking me into it. It's been . . . nice . . . to have some time off to just relax for a few days." He breathed deeply and looked out at the ocean. "This was just what I didn't know I needed."

Tessa nodded. "You should do it regularly. You know, at least once a year. I mean, I'm not sure if you're aware of this, but there are people who actually take time off work for leisure activities sometimes."

Silas scoffed. "Blasphemy!"

They both dissolved into giggles.

They didn't walk too far since Tessa was on a time constraint, but the conversation was easy. Tessa didn't think about Timothy or Mr. Blade. She was in the moment as they watched the sunset together, carrying their sandals so their toes could sink into the sand.

Back in front of the hotel, Tessa faced Silas. "I'll see you at the airport tomorrow, I guess." She felt bummed that vacation time was almost over.

But did it have to be? They were going back to the same place, after all. The same building, in fact. Tessa and Silas would see each other every day, like they had since Tessa moved into Mist River Manor.

Maybe this didn't have to be the end of their budding romance—because Tessa had to admit to herself now that's what it was. She had feelings for Silas, for sure, and he'd given off all the signals that it was reciprocal.

He leaned forward, brushing her cheek with his fingers. "Right," he said softly, "I'll see you at the airport."

His lips brushed hers lightly, just for an instant, and then he winked and walked into the gathering darkness.

It had happened so fast Tessa could almost convince herself it had been in her imagination. Except it hadn't. Silas had kissed her.

And it had been wonderful. A little short. But wonderful.

A smile played on her lips as she touched the spot where his had brushed them.

But as Tessa entered the hotel and saw a crowd of reapers passing through the lobby toward the conference room, Tessa's elation abruptly soured. She'd almost forgotten.

How could she have a romantic relationship with Silas? Either she'd have to lie to him about her job, which was bound to end in feelings of betrayal at some point, or tell him about it, which could be dangerous for her and the other reapers.

No. As much as she didn't want to, Tessa was going to have to find a way to break things off with Silas. For both of their sakes.

Chapter 18

"You look like somebody stole your puppy and replaced it with a big sack of stinky trash," Gloria said.

Tessa laughed. "That's . . . a strangely detailed and odd scenario."

Gloria shrugged. "Well, it's the truth. That's exactly the face I'd expect you to make if such a thing happened. It *didn't* happen, did it?"

"No!" Tessa laughed again.

"Then what's wrong?"

"Nothing." She sank into a chair in the conference room.

"Definitely *not* a nothing face." Gloria tipped her head, examining Tessa closer. "That's a *something* expression if I ever saw one. Did you have a fight with your hottie landlord?"

"No!"

"But the face *is* about hottie landlord, isn't it? I have a knack for these kinds of things."

"Being nosey?" Tessa frowned and sank deeper into the chair. "Okay . . . maybe."

Gloria simply continued to stare expectantly at her.

"Fine," Tessa huffed. "I'm going to tell him we can't be together when we get home. I don't want to do it. But it's better for everyone if I do it now instead of letting it drag out until I hurt his feelings even worse."

"How would you do that?"

"By continuing to lie to him every day about what I do."

Gloria's chest rose and fell as she sighed deeply. "You're a slow learner, you know that?"

Tessa scowled at her friend. "Am not."

"Are too." Gloria looked like she was going to say more, but someone tapped on the microphone, drawing their attention.

It was Cheryl.

"Am not," Tessa added triumphantly. She perked up, sitting straighter, wondering why her mother was speaking.

With a huge smile that made her look a tiny bit like a Mr. Ed, Cheryl lifted her hands wide and cooed into the microphone, "Thank you all for being here. Both tonight and at the conference in general. What a year. And that's what we're here to celebrate. Not the conference, but the year of reaping."

Everyone cheered and clapped.

"But, as with all lovely things, this one is at an end. It's time for us to celebrate the camaraderie we've had and the things we've learned." She clasped her hands together and grinned like she'd just watched her offspring graduate from law school. She'd made no secret of the fact she wanted Tessa to be a high-powered lawyer. Nor had she hid her disappointment when Tessa announced that she had no intention of doing any such thing.

Cheryl continued, "I'm so proud of this community and everything we do. To that end, it's time for our annual awards ceremony."

The excitement was palpable in the room. Tessa realized this was a big deal for the reapers.

"Most of you know how we like to do these things. We start off a little silly—a little reminiscent of the high school yearbook. These were added when Lee was in charge of the awards."

"They're based off *The Office*, not the high school yearbook," he called out.

Cheryl rolled her eyes. "First, we have an award for the best-dressed reaper. Now, I'd like to remind you that these awards are decided on by committee, not by me." Cheryl placed a hand on her chest. "So, I am not the one to blame if you weren't chosen! Remember, you have a whole year to plan a better wardrobe to try and win next year."

Everyone laughed.

Tessa was amazed. Cheryl was gracious and funny. Everyone was engaged and enjoying themselves with her at the mic. How had that even happened? Cheryl wasn't scheduled to be at the conference. This must be an impromptu thing for her.

Was Timothy supposed to emcee the award ceremony?

But Cheryl was opening an envelope, so Tessa had to pay attention. The room fell silent as she read a sheet inside and smiled. "Well. I will have to accept this award on behalf of the recipient, who is otherwise occupied at this time." She held up the slip of paper. "The winner is Bubba!"

Everyone clapped and cheered.

Cheryl held up a hand. "I would like to interject here that, as deserving as Bubba is of this award, we all know he'd give it up in a heartbeat to the reaper who truly dressed like no one else and won this award six times in past years—Art. We will all miss him."

Applause rang through the room. Cheryl let it die down naturally before she continued. "The next award is for longest serving reaper." She opened the envelope and then scanned the crowd as she announced, "Shirley!"

Shirley made her way to the front to accept a small plaque amid whistles and cheers. She said a quiet thank you into the microphone before heading back to her seat.

"Another of Lee's additions. Next up is our award for most likely to be late for a reap." Cheryl opened the envelope and Tessa held her breath. How embarrassing would it be if her name was on there?

But when Cheryl looked up, she announced, "The winner is Colton."

A reaper Tessa had only met in passing went up to get his plaque, red-faced as everyone jeered at him from the crowd. Tessa blew out a relieved breath and vowed to make it to all of her future reaps on time. She never wanted to be given that award at the yearly conference.

"And next we have the rookie of the year award. This one truly is a honor to hand out. I know I still have mine sitting proudly on a bookshelf beside my desk. Gloria has hers. I'd be lying if I didn't tell you that I'm hoping to see three of these around the office." Now Tessa squirmed with fervor. Her mother would probably embarrass her on stage. She opened the envelope and sighed. "Lydia."

Lydia, not quite as red-faced as Colton, took her prize.

"And finally," Cheryl said, "the most talked-about and competed-for award for the district supervisor whose district had the greatest number of allotments this year." Cheryl opened the envelope, expression pleasantly tense as she read. Then she smiled. "The winner this year is Lee Stuart, by only three allocations."

Shouts and boos went up from western and eastern reapers, respectively. As Lee made his way forward to accept the silver trophy from Cheryl, Tessa's gaze swept the crowd and landed on April in the front row. The gray-haired woman was clearly seething. If her eyes had been able to make lightning, it was clear she would have burned Lee down right that second.

Lee shook Cheryl's hand, and she stepped aside for him to speak into the microphone. "Thank you so much, Cheryl. And thanks to my team, the western division, for bringing me this honor once again." He pinned Cheryl with a smile. "I know the eastern district worked hard, and they only fell short by such a tiny bit. I think this is the closest it's been in years. Last year, we beat you by five. Way to narrow the margin." He clucked his tongue. "But better luck next year."

April's hands fisted on the desk in front of her. Her expression darkened even more.

Tessa worried April might leap up and try to strangle Lee. Cheryl kept an eye on April too, as though worried her boss may blow a figurative gasket and literally explode into an angry tirade.

Tessa thought the whole thing was silly. Three allocations. That was nothing in the grand scheme of reaps done over the past year. Why make such a fuss about it? And who decided how the things were split? She guessed it was on merit, on who was doing the best job. Otherwise, it made no sense.

Lee finished his speech, and Cheryl said some final uplifting things that no one listened to as they all buzzed about the allotment award. Cheryl concluded by wishing everyone a safe trip home.

Gloria turned toward Tessa. "One last bar night?"

But Tessa shook her head. Something had stuck in her mind while Lee was speaking. She watched April exit the conference room, ignoring anyone who tried to speak to her. Tessa got to her feet. "You know what? I have something to do real fast. I'll meet you after I'm done, okay?"

Gloria shrugged. "Sure."

Tessa headed into the lobby and waited for the elevator. Inside, she punched the button for the sixth floor.

Three allocations. Lee had won by three. And there had been three since they got on the plane in Chicago—Art, Cynthia, and the man on the golf course. Dani would have been another if Tessa hadn't saved her.

No one knew who had reaped Art and Cynthia. They were eastern district reapers, but could they somehow have been counted in the western district's numbers?

Of course, there were always people being reaped. Every minute of the day. But Art and Cynthia were unaccounted for, and that was unusual.

The third reap on her mind—the man who had the stroke—seemed to have been allocated to the eastern district, but was it?

The reap hadn't felt right to Tessa, just like Dani's death hadn't. Still, Lydia had done the reap, so it had to have been allocated to the east, right?

Tessa needed to talk to Timothy.

When she got out of the elevator on the sixth floor, Tessa stood for a minute, looking both ways and wondering where they were keeping Timothy. Cheryl had said there wasn't much going on up there, and she was right. The hallway was empty.

Tessa stood uncertainly and chewed her bottom lip. *Which way?* She shrugged. If she had to check every room, so be it.

But as she took a step to the left, a sound stopped her. She whirled around. It had been a laugh. And she recognized it.

Tessa hurried in the direction of the sound, glad when it rang out again to help her pinpoint where to go. She arrived at a closed doorway at the end of the hall. She pressed her ear to the door, and it wasn't long before she heard Bubba laugh again. She knocked softly.

Bubba pulled the door open and looked surprised. "Oh, hey, Tessa. Did your mom send you up for something?"

She shook her head. "Can I talk to Timothy for a minute?"

His brow scrunched. "I don't know." He glanced over his shoulder into the room at something she couldn't see.

"It'll just take a minute, I promise. I want to ask him something."

Bubba shrugged and opened the door wider. "I guess it's okay. Nobody told me he couldn't have visitors. And he has the cuffs on. They'll stop him if he tries to do anything weird."

"Thanks." Tessa followed Bubba in, closing the door behind her. It was a regular hotel room with two beds. An old comedy played on the TV.

Timothy, who had been lying on one of the beds, rolled onto his elbow and pushed himself up. His hair and clothes were rumpled, lapel stained as usual. He looked miserable.

"Hey, there." She sat on the foot of the bed, more than arm's length away from him. "How are you holding up?"

He shook his head. "Not so great, actually."

"I can understand that. Listen, for what it's worth, I don't really think you're guilty."

His gaze met hers. "That's worth a lot. Thanks."

"I was just at the awards ceremony, and Lee won by three allocations. I was thinking about that. How many allocations were the numbers off by before the conference? You know, when you and April went to Chicago to investigate it."

"Four," he answered.

Four. Did that make sense?

Dani . . .

Her mind whirled as puzzle pieces slotted together. She thought about the rivalry between April and Lee. How some said they'd both go to any length to outdo each other. Tessa had thought that was hyperbole, but maybe it wasn't. At least for one of them.

"Well, my shift is over." Bubba got up and headed for the door. "Tessa, you coming with me or staying here?"

The three mis-allocations were exactly the ones Lee needed to win the award. Which meant April wasn't the killer at all.

Bubba opened the door. "Ah! You're right on time. Thanks for relieving me."

A slither made its way up Tessa's spine as she realized who must be behind the murders of the two reapers.

The same person who had just arrived to take Bubba's place. Who had entered the room and closed the door. Who stood smiling at her, oozing charm.

Lee Stuart.

Chapter 19

A quick glance at Timothy let Tessa know she was right about Lee. Or at least that he'd come to the same conclusion as she had. The assistant's face lost its color, and he shrank back against the headboard as though trying to blend in with it.

Lee's gaze moved from Tessa to Timothy and back. A slow smile raised the corners of his mouth, and he reached over to lock the deadbolt.

Tessa's mind raced as she tried to figure out how to get out of the predicament. She decided the best thing to do was to keep her mouth shut—act like she hadn't put things together. In theory, it'd work because there were still several facets she'd yet to understand.

If she could convince Lee she was harmless, maybe he'd let her go. And then, she could find her mother, or, even better, Mr. Blade.

"Well, well. What do we have here?" Lee's smile grew broader. "A gathering of the minds? Fraternizing with the enemy? You're aware this man is charged with, well, serious charges. It could even be viewed as murder in a certain light."

"I didn't do it. Tessa knows I didn't do it."

"Does she now?" Lee leaned back against the door, crossing his arms and ankles. "And who does she suppose did?"

Unfortunately for Tessa and the solid, safe plan, the connection between her brain and mouth was, as usual, broken. Her brain was unable to stop her mouth from blurting out, "It was you. You killed Art. And Cynthia. Didn't you? And probably more."

She winced.

Timothy winced.

Come on, mouth. Work with me here. "Why, though?" Clearly, her mouth had gone rogue, and Tessa would just have to roll with it.

"It was all part of the game."

"Game? Taking people's lives—before they're supposed to go—is a game for you?" Rage boiled up in her chest, and she spat out, "Little Dani's life . . . her death . . . that's a *game* to you?"

Lee chuckled. "We take lives every day. That's what we do. There are so many people on this earth. No one really notices a few extras gone."

"Besides their families, their friends—"

"Their coworkers," Lee finished. "That's why you stuck your nose in it. All for a couple of people you barely even met."

Tessa balled her fists. She wanted to leap on the evil man and throttle him with her bare hands. But she forced herself to breathe deeply and stay seated, reminding herself that he was dangerous.

She glanced at Timothy. His eyes were wide.

"It was all for the contest, wasn't it?" Tessa accused.

"My rivalry with April has gotten more heated every year," he conceded. "Not only do we spar over the award, but we also place personal bets on various other things." His eyes slid to Timothy. "Including mythical death allotments."

Timothy looked like he was going to be sick.

It looked like Tessa would have to win this fight alone. She only hoped he kept it together. If she was going to die in here by Lee's hands, she didn't want it to be beside vomit.

Lee shook his head, still looking amused. "In an orderly world, the allotments would be about equal between our two divisions—barring a natural disaster or something, of course. But this world isn't ordered. It's dirty and rough and competitive. People who understand that and give in to the natural order of things will always do better than those who don't—goody-two-shoes like the both of you."

Tessa's eyebrows went up. Timothy looked away from Lee.

"Yes, that's right." Lee's hard gaze pinned Timothy. "I know you were working against me."

Timothy didn't answer, but a muscle clenched in his jaw.

"I don't understand," Tessa interjected. "How did Art's and Cynthia's deaths count for you? They lived in the eastern division. They died in the eastern division."

"Well, that was my trick, of course. It was actually April who discovered the loophole, but she never understood it well enough to manipulate. Luckily, I was able to grasp the finer points and use it to my advantage.

"You see, if a death is cheated somehow . . . the person doesn't die as they were destined to . . . that allocation is up in the air, to do with as anyone pleases. I just have to use my managerial access to the reaper app, add the unused allocation number, and optionally the victim, then be the first to take it off the queue."

"All I had to do was prevent a few eastern deaths and voila! They became allotments for me. I figured I could use them to my advantage twice—once to add to my side's total and help me win the award, and once to remove a couple of April's best reapers from the equation. Doing that could help me win for years to come."

"But how do you manage to prevent those deaths? Doesn't their reaper see you intervene?"

"Ah. Now you're using your noggin." He pushed himself away from the door and started pacing in front it, a few steps in each direction. He reminded Tessa of a professor giving a lecture. "They didn't see me for the same reason no one saw me take Art or Cynthia across the veil." He gave Tessa a sly, sidelong look. "Because I received secret knowledge from the original reaper. A secret I can tap into at will. I can become invisible."

"Corwin Blade gave you the ability to go invisible?" Tessa was shocked.

"It was many years ago. Long before I was the western district supervisor. He said I was a promising reaper. So promising that I deserved a special gift."

Promising. The word rang in Tessa's mind. Blade had said something like that to Tessa at the pool.

Tessa's mind kept scrambling to keep up. "Okay, you showed up and prevented three deaths from occurring in April's territory—"

"Four deaths," Timothy corrected. "I caught on after the first two. He wasn't fast enough to take the other two from the app. I took them as soon as I saw the allotment, then gave the first two Lydia. That's why I followed her. I was hoping to figure what was going on—because even her reap went to him."

"The invisibility," Lee sneered. "She only thought she did that reap. I was guiding that man along the whole time."

"And Dani?"

"It was nothing personal." Lee cleared his throat. "After the first two, with Timothy hot on my trail and you snooping around, I knew I could no longer choose my victims from the reaper community. I had to venture out. I let the app decide."

It seemed like Lee was getting bored of talking. Tessa wanted to keep him talking. Maybe, just maybe, Cheryl would be looking for her. And maybe, just maybe, she'd come up here.

"You know, there's still Dani's allotment unaccounted for." He reached into the back of his waistband and pulled something out. "And lucky for me, I was just plugging it into my phone on the elevator." He brandished a blade in front of his body, pointing first at Tessa with it and then at Timothy. Then, with his other hand, he pulled out his phone. "The only remaining question is who the lucky one will be. Stabbed to death. What a way to go."

Timothy choked out a mini-sob and shrank further back against the headboard. Tessa glanced at him before retraining her eyes on Lee's knife. She knew Timothy wouldn't be able to fight Lee much if at all. His hands were bound by the magical invisible handcuffs. If they were both going to get out of this alive, it was Tessa who was going to have to make it happen.

Lee's knife seemed to quiver indecisively for a second before it settled on Tessa. "Maybe it's finally your time to go, Ms. Randolph. After all, you've already cheated death once. You can't do that forever."

"That debt has already been paid," Tessa ground out, thinking of her father taking her place—dying so she didn't have to when she was a teenager. No way was she going to let this maniac make it so his sacrifice was for nothing.

Slowly, she got to her feet, keeping the bed between her and Lee.

"Be that as it may," Lee said, "I can see you have an annoying rebellious streak. Timothy here will be easier for me to control. I'm sure we can work out an agreement, can't we Tim? May I call you Tim?"

"No."

"Come on. It will be nice to have someone in April's office who's under my thumb. I'd like to smoke her out of the water by dozens of allocations next year. That will be much easier if I have an operative working right under her nose." He stepped around the end of the bed toward Tessa, gripping the knife hard and still fidgeting with the app, attempting to type with one thumb. "Yes. I think today is *your* unlucky day."

As Lee moved in front of a big mirror on the wall, his reflection caught Tessa's eye for a moment. Only it wasn't only his reflection. There was another person visible there.

Blade.

She jerked her head to look for the man in the room, but he wasn't there.

Once again, Tessa thought of their conversation by the pool. What had he said? That the power of the scythe was hers to use as needed. She had only to wish for it.

She hadn't understood at the time that he meant it literally. But Lee's confession that the Grim Reaper had given him access to invisibility had made it clear to her.

Lee kept moving. He kept drawing closer, distracted by the phone.

All of a sudden, Timothy, who had apparently used his blubbering and weeping as a cover to disguise the fact that he'd maneuvered himself into a crouched position with his feet under him, propelled himself forward across the bed, hurling his body to intercept Lee.

Lee grabbed Timothy's arm and used the assistant's momentum to send him hurtling through the air. But in doing so, dropped the phone.

Timothy screamed as the blade glanced off him before he hit the dresser and crashed to the ground with a sickening thud.

Tessa glanced his direction, not wanting to take her eyes off Lee for long. Blood pooled under Timothy's body. She fought the urge to rush to him, forcing her gaze back to Lee.

Timothy had stopped him, at least for a moment. Lee's eyes were on Timothy and the blood too. But the assistant's spirit didn't rise out of his body. He wasn't dead. Yet.

Tessa took the second of Lee's inattention to plant her feet shoulder-length apart and brace for his inevitable attack.

She squared her shoulders and focused on Lee. "Turn yourself in," she said. "Tell the task force what you did and face the consequences. You can still have a life if you end this now."

Lee dragged his gaze over to her. He threw back his head and howled with laughter. When he brought his chin down again, the look in his eye was chilling. He held the knife up higher. "I do have a life. The exact one I want. I'm number one. Invincible. I'm as close to the original Grim Reaper as it comes. I choose who lives and who dies. And I choose you to die."

Tessa had less than a moment to react when Lee charged forward. She raised her hand, thinking of Blade and the scythe he'd mentioned. When the wickedly sharp, curved blade appeared in her hand, its wooden handle smooth, as though someone had spent hours sanding it to perfection, she was so surprised she almost dropped it. She fumbled for a moment and then slapped the other hand onto the handle to steady it. She lifted the blade.

Lee's face registered complete shock but then he looked resigned. "I see I'm not the only one the boss let in on a secret."

"I think the boss has decided you're unhinged and need to go."

He shook his head, bringing the knife forward and pointing it at Tessa's neck. "Nah. I still think my secret is better than yours."

And, suddenly, she couldn't see him anymore. Lee and the knife were both gone.

Tessa twirled in a circle, but Lee wasn't there. It was as though he had completely disappeared from the room.

But she knew that wasn't the case. He was still there, stalking her with his knife, looking for a chance to plunge it into her neck.

Tessa brought the scythe up and tried to keep moving. She didn't want to create a still, motionless target for the psychopath.

Timothy moaned and stirred, but Tessa didn't spare any attention for him. She'd have to hope Lee came after her instead of deciding to take out the easier target——the injured man who didn't even know the reaper was there.

The comforter moved a tiny bit at the foot of the bed. Tessa swung the scythe, hard, in that direction. But it didn't connect with anything. Instead, the momentum of her swing spun her ninety degrees to the left.

Panic tore at the edges of her mind as she anticipated an invisible Lee grabbing her while she tried to get her balance.

She stumbled and had to let go of the scythe with her left hand to steady herself on the bed.

When she looked up again, movement caught her eye. Her gaze popped over to the mirror. It was Lee. She could see him in the mirror. He wasn't completely solid. More like a ghost that she could see better in her periphery than straight-on. But she could see him behind her, lifting his knife over her back.

Without thinking about it, Tessa whirled, using both hands on the scythe as she swung it like a bat.

It sliced right through Lee's body.

It felt like cutting butter.

And Lee was solid again.

He had only a fraction of a second to give Tessa a shocked look before he crumpled to the ground at her feet, the knife clattering out of his hand.

"I'm not dying today, Mr. Stuart," Tessa said. "Today, you fill Dani's allotment yourself." The scythe was gone. She glanced at the mirror, where Blade's reflection had appeared again. He grinned and winked. And then he was gone.

She skirted around Lee, rushing to kneel next to Timothy. He stirred, and she helped him sit up. A deep cut on his arm seeped blood slowly. "You'll be okay," she assured him. "I'll get help."

"Tessa!" Timothy grabbed her arm. His eyes were focused over her shoulder. "Look!"

She twisted her neck to see what Timothy pointed at. Lee's soul ascended from his ruined body. The spirit looked around, first at his own body, and then at them. His ghostly face twisted in disgust.

Tessa popped to her feet. She waved a hand to open a path to the other side. Bright light shone, as though from the ceiling. She headed toward Lee's spirit, intending to tether it and take it across the veil. She'd seen Gloria do it once and thought it looked simple enough.

But Lee smiled widely. Shook his head. Then, he took off.

Before Tessa could do anything, the spirit had passed right through the closed hotel room door.

He'd escaped.

Chapter 20

By the time Tessa managed to wrench the door open, the hallway was empty. There was no sign of Lee's spirit.

She gritted her teeth. "No. This isn't happening again." She spun around, rushed back into the room, and knelt by Timothy. "I don't know how to get these cuffs off." She worked quickly, using a case hastily torn off its pillow as a tourniquet for his arm. "Stay here and I'll send help."

He pinned her with a pointed look. "Catch that jerk and send him on to his next life!"

"I will." She patted his arm and took off, pulling out her phone as she raced to the elevator. She tapped at the screen and then held it to her ear. "Come on, come on. Answer," she muttered as she got on the elevator and punched the button for the first floor.

"Theresa? Where are you? You disappeared from the awards ceremony so fast I didn't get to talk to you." Cheryl's voice was clear and calm. It anchored Tessa a bit, helping to get her heart slowed down.

"It . . . it was Lee Stuart," she said, finally catching her breath. "He's the one behind Art and Cynthia's deaths. And more."

"He—he did what?"

"He saved people slotted to die in the east, so the allotments went to his side. Then, he used them to kill people who weren't really scheduled to die." She tapped her foot and watched the light indicate which level she was on. The elevator seemed to be moving slower than usual—they always do.

"But how do you know that?"

"Because he told me right before I . . . before I . . ."

"Spit it out!" her mother scolded.

"Before I reaped him."

There was silence on the line. If Tessa wasn't so wound up about finding Lee, she might have celebrated the victory of driving her mother speechless. She couldn't remember having ever accomplished that before.

But she *was* distracted by the matter at hand and didn't have time to bask. "Mom. Lee's dead. And his spirit escaped. I don't even know if he's still in the hotel. I'm going down to the main floor to try and spot him."

"Okay. It's just a lot to process. Even for me."

"It's not all," Tessa replied. "Timothy is up in that room where the task force was keeping him. He's injured. He needs help right away."

"I'll go up there now. You find Lee. There are plenty of reapers to help. Be careful." Cheryl hung up without waiting for Tessa to respond.

The elevator door finally opened, and Tessa hurried out. There were a few people in the lobby, and one of them was Bubba. His expression was bewildered as he focused on Tessa. "Lee Stuart just passed right through my body. What happened? Did Timothy kill him too?"

"No. I did."

Bubba's confusion deepened.

She waved a hand before Bubba could say anything else. "I don't have time to explain. Which way did Lee go? We have to catch him and cross him over."

He spun around and pointed. "I think toward the bar."

Tessa ran past Bubba, dodging around other reapers in the lobby and hallway until she skidded to a stop in the bar's doorway. Frustration boiled up in her chest as she surveyed the place—there were so many reapers there that it was hard to sort out who was who. A spirit would be difficult to spot in the dim room with all the live people milling about.

Bubba arrived next to her, also scanning the room. "I don't see him."

"Me either."

"Let me ask around. Maybe someone saw him go through." Bubba hurried forward.

Tessa moved into the room, making her way around reapers and trying to look everywhere at once for Lee.

"There you are! Do you want a margarita or a gin and tonic?" Gloria blocked Tessa's path. She had a cocktail in her hand and a wide smile on her face. "One last party before we head back to the grind."

Tessa shook her head. "I can't." She took Gloria's glass and set it on a nearby table. "Actually, you can't either. I need your help."

"Hey! That was expensive." Then Gloria snorted out a laugh and waved a hand. "But whatever. I put it on the black card. What's up?"

"Lee Stuart murdered Art and Cynthia. And a few other people. Actually, who knows how many people he's killed over the years." Tessa looked over her friend's shoulder, trying to spot Lee's spirit. She scanned the area near the ceiling but didn't find him.

Chet was one thing. But battling a spirit with the reaper knowledge Lee possessed was going to be difficult. What would happen if he really got away? She didn't want to think about it.

Gloria looked puzzled. "You mean, Lee was killing people who weren't scheduled to die?"

"That's exactly what I mean. And now he's dead. But his spirit escaped, and I have to find it and cross it over. I need all the help I can get."

She felt a burst of friendship when Gloria immediately took on a professional air and started scanning the room for Lee.

"Tessa!" Bubba arrived next to the two women. "No one I talked to saw Lee."

Tessa groaned. "Okay. Where else could he be?" She paused as a sudden thought came to her. "And why would he have come to the bar in the first place? I mean, there are so many reapers here. If his intention is to escape being crossed over, you'd think he'd stay as far away from reapers who could see him and take him over the veil as possible." Her mind raced to catch up with its own train of thought. "Unless escape isn't his intention."

"I'm not sure I follow." Gloria and Bubba exchanged a confused look.

"Maybe he's after April. You know, for one last opportunity to one-up her." Tessa leaned forward. "Can a spirit kill a live person?"

Gloria's brow creased as she considered the question. "I've heard of it happening. I think there have to be certain extenuating circumstances. But Lee was a district supervisor. If anyone knows the loopholes, it would probably be him." She paused. "You think he's going to try to *kill* April?"

"I think we have to assume he is." Tessa spun around again, this time scanning the room for the eastern district supervisor. "Have either of you seen April?"

"Did you say you're looking for April?" Shirley spoke from the table next to them, where she'd commandeered Gloria's drink and sucked down half of it already. "I think she went to take one last dip in the pool. You know she's quite the swimmer."

"The pool. Come on." Tessa took off for the door, Gloria and Bubba right behind her.

As they rushed through the lobby, the elevator doors opened, and Cheryl came out, supporting a sagging Timothy.

"Mom! We haven't found Lee yet. I think he's after April—at the pool."

"April!" Timothy was pale, and he cradled his injured arm with the other one. "No! We have to stop him." He started in the direction of the courtyard pool but stumbled over his own feet.

Cheryl caught him. "You're not stopping anyone. I'm taking you to the hospital." She pulled him gently toward the door. Over her shoulder, she said, "Lee is probably a pretty powerful spirit. He had a lot of reaper secrets when he was alive. Don't underestimate him."

Her mother's words sent a chill through Tessa, and she ran faster, losing Bubba while Gloria struggled to keep up in her heels.

"Remember the tether I taught you?" Gloria asked.

"I do."

"You got this."

Gloria stopped abruptly and slipped off her shoes while Tessa kept on. She erupted onto the pool deck and then slid to a stop, trying to make sense of what she saw.

No one was there except April, who was in the pool, lazily doing a slow backstroke, eyes fixed above her as she tracked her way across the pool.

There was no Lee, and Tessa felt a flash of relief. They'd been wrong. He wasn't after April.

She heard someone else arrive and glanced over her shoulder to see that Gloria had made it. She panted, eyes on April before moving to Tessa. "She's okay," she said.

"Yeah."

A splash drew Tessa's attention back to the pool. April was no longer on the surface. She had dived down.

That was strange. It had really looked like she was doing backstroke laps. And there was an awful lot of water churning for a peaceful underwater swim.

Tessa moved to the edge of pool so she could see April better. The supervisor was twisting in the water, not simply swimming. Her hands and feet flapped wildly as she strained to get back to the surface. But something seemed to be preventing it.

Then Tessa saw it—there were extra hands down there. Ghostly ones that were hard to see in the splashing water. But once she spotted them, the rest of Lee's spirit-body quickly came into focus. Somehow, he was holding onto April. Keeping her from going up for air.

How was he doing that?

But it didn't matter how. He was doing it—Lee was powerful in death as he had been in life, just like Cheryl warned. And April probably only had a few moments more to live.

She didn't have time to say anything to Gloria or Bubba, who had finally arrived too. She just kicked off her shoes and jumped into the pool without thinking.

Tessa silently thanked her parents for their dogged belief that, when you lived in Michigan, water proficiency was a must. They'd put her through years of swimming lessons, and she was pretty good at it.

She swam as fast as possible to the spot where Lee and April fought, having no idea what the plan was once she arrived. The secret of the scythe wouldn't help her against someone who was already dead.

Lee's spirit turned its head and spotted her. His face twisted into unmitigated rage, and he roared in anger. The sound came through the water and seemed to have the physical oomph to push Tessa away.

She fought the water pressure to continue forward, straining to reach April. The water churned and rolled, both from the frantic movements of April's body and from whatever Lee was doing to make it worse.

Tessa couldn't see much. Without goggles or a face mask, the chlorine made her eyes burn. She shut them tight and surged forward, throwing caution to the wind because April had very little time left.

Her fingertips brushed skin, and Tessa clamped down on April's arm. She used the other hand and both feet to propel herself upward. Lee's inhuman roar pounded in her ears along with the water.

It felt like April was made of rocks. Lee was somehow applying more pressure downward than she could apply upward. There was no way Tessa would be able to pull her to the surface. She knew there would come a moment when she'd have to decide between letting the other woman go or taking in water herself. She firmly clamped down on the thought and kicked madly.

Suddenly, April began moving upward. Her body was still extra heavy, but it was a little better. Tessa snuck a look through squinting eyes and saw Gloria on April's other side. She was helping. Then Bubba appeared in front of them. He grabbed April under the arms and all four of them surged for the surface.

As soon as her face broke through the water, Tessa dragged in air. Beside her, April did too, but then she immediately began coughing. "Take her! Get her out!" Tessa gasped, pushing April toward the other two reapers. She spun in a circle, looking for Lee.

It didn't take long to find him. Apparently, he wasn't interested in fleeing. He was right next to her, his snarling spirit face just inches in front of hers.

"It's over, Lee. Time to go." She treaded water with one hand while opening a portal with the other.

"I'll take you with me. I'll take you all with me." His ghostly face was so twisted with rage that he looked like a caricature of a devil from some old Renaissance painting.

"Wow. You're a really unpleasant dude, you know that? But I'm not going to let that happen." She glanced up at the bright light from the portal above them. Only it didn't look the way it usually did. Instead of the standard tunnel, with warm yellow lighting, it was darker. Creepier. "Looks like you're heading to a special spot across the veil, though. I'm sure you'll have just as much fun there as you tried to have here."

Lee glanced up, and his expression morphed from furious to fearful.

Tessa took the moment of inattention to pull on her reaper powers and produce a tether. She caught Lee in it easily. Shocked, he writhed and shouted. But he couldn't go anywhere. He was trapped.

Above them, a figure appeared in the portal. A tall dark man stood there, his shoulder-length hair waving as though there were a slight breeze. Blade nodded approvingly at Tessa and then turned a frown on Lee. He reached out and grabbed the district manager's spirit and made a yanking motion.

Suddenly, Lee was standing in the portal with Blade, the fear etched even deeper into his spirit features.

Tessa was relieved to be able to use both hands to stay afloat again as she watched the two men disappear across the veil, Lee screaming wordlessly the whole way.

Chapter 21

"I miss the hotel pool. And the bar." Gloria rested her chin on folded arms on the desk. She sighed deeply. "But not the murder and mayhem."

Tessa leaned on the door jamb of Gloria's office. "There's a pool at my apartment building."

"And a hottie landlord," Gloria shot back. "You two can pick right up where you left off in Miami."

"We'll see. I haven't decided yet." Tessa shrugged. "In the meantime, we could keep living as though we're on vacation. You know—after work. Heaven knows Mist River has enough bars to keep us busy every evening for a year. I mean, as long as we stay away from Frank's."

Gloria sat up, her expression brightening. "That's a great idea. Although I wouldn't want to put a damper on you and hottie's relationship."

Tessa opened her mouth to argue, but Cheryl's voice calling for her cut off her train of thought.

Why was she so intent on cutting off her relationship with Silas? In Miami, it seemed logical. But here in Mist River, where things were comfortably mundane, she was failing to remember the key points.

Gloria waved Tessa away. "Better see what the boss wants."

With a grin, Tessa crossed the lobby to her mother's office. Cheryl sat at the desk watching her computer screen, through which voices floated. Tessa moved to stand behind her mother so she could see the monitor. April and Timothy were on video call. Timothy's arm was bandaged, but his coloring was back to normal. There was an unidentified purple food stain on the white gauze wrapping that made Tessa smile.

When he saw Tessa come into view, Timothy waved. "There you are. I wanted to say thank you for everything you did."

She waved back. "I should be thanking *you*. You saved my life when you prevented Lee from finishing that allotment on his phone in that hotel room. You were really brave."

Timothy puffed up visibly. "Nah. I'm just a guy who likes numbers. And Lee Stuart was always messing them up. Jerk."

Tessa smiled again. "Which is why you followed Lydia to that stroke victim. If you hadn't, I'm not sure we could've put the pieces together so easily."

He nodded. "Even then, I couldn't narrow it down to Lee. His invisibility made things difficult. But my time in handcuffs ignoring the very bad comedies Bubba liked to watch allowed me to put more together." He leaned toward the camera. "You did great when I sent you on that reap in Miami. By then, I'd figured out those were extra reaps somehow. I knew those people weren't supposed to die, but I couldn't risk telling anyone. And I sent you because I knew you were as after the truth as I was. I figured you'd refuse to do the reap if it felt wrong." He grinned and sat back again. "I was right."

She chuckled and glanced at Cheryl. Was it Tessa's imagination, or did her mother look a little bit proud?

"I owe you my thanks too." April's voice was soft but her tone earnest. "We've never had such a terrible convention. And I feel partially to blame. Our rivalry was always something, but I never for the life of me thought Lee would go so far. So dark."

Tessa nodded. "You're welcome."

"Really. If you hadn't found me in the pool exactly when you did—and if you hadn't jumped in without thinking of your own safety—I wouldn't be here. Lee's spirit would have killed me for sure. And he'd probably still be roaming the earth, causing problems for the task force." She glanced at Timothy.

He nodded. "Turns out Lee had more allocations to fill than he let on. He could have gone on quite the poltergeisterly killing spree." Timothy's mouth twisted in disgust.

"What about that? The numbers, I mean. How can they be made right now?" Tessa hoped Timothy wasn't going to say that a bunch of people had to be chosen to die.

"The big man himself, Mr. Blade, fixed that up," Timothy said. "A message came through from him this morning. He's rebalanced the allotments, and we're starting from scratch. By the way. That was some trick you did in that hotel room. Nice secret Mr. Blade gave you."

Tessa's eyes darted toward Cheryl again, but her mother kept her gaze on the computer screen. "Yeah. Well. I'm glad you're both okay."

"Back at ya," Timothy said with a smile.

April grinned and cut off the video.

Tessa sat on the edge of Cheryl's desk. "They looked good. I'm glad that's all over."

Cheryl tipped her head, regarding Tessa. "It's an awesome and terrible thing to receive a secret from Mr. Blade," she said in a calm but slightly ominous tone.

Tessa shifted her weight, suddenly both physically and mentally uncomfortable. "Um. Okay." She didn't know what her mother was trying to say, but it didn't matter. She never planned to summon the scythe again. There shouldn't be any need for her to. But there *was* something she'd been wondering about. She figured it was as good a time as any to ask. "How many secrets are there? And how many reapers have one?"

The corners of Cheryl's mouth twitched upward. "We can't be sure how many there are. And there aren't many of us entrusted with them. But those of us who *have them* must guard our secret closely. Use it wisely. Or we risk becoming like Lee Stuart—twisted by its great power."

Tessa's back straightened. Had Cheryl said *we*? "Wait, do *you* have—"

Cheryl interrupted. "You did well in Florida, dear. It's time to get back to work now that we're home. Check your app—you have an assignment in thirty minutes."

"But . . ."

Cheryl waved a hand. "I have another conference call to attend. There's a lot to do to make up for losing a district manager—and a task force member. I'm sure I don't have time for any more small talk." She clicked at the keyboard, clearly having dismissed her daughter.

Tessa felt a wave of frustration. It seemed like, no matter how much she tried to get Cheryl to open up to her—to share things so they could be closer—her mother just closed off more. She longed for a better relationship. She longed for her mother to trust her. Which reminded her. "Mom, why didn't I get one of the black cards?"

"Ooooh." Cheryl sighed. "Right." She jotted something on a notepad. "I have to send in those expense reports. Yet another thing I have to get done today. Punishment for taking a day off."

"Mom." Tessa glared.

Cheryl leaned back in her seat and did a sort of twirling motion with her hand. "Theresa, I did give you a card. It's in an envelope on your desk. You must've missed seeing it before you left."

Tessa was confident her mother was not telling the truth. Or the envelope had been misplaced. But she couldn't argue until she'd done a thorough check.

She remembered what Bryce Hanson had told her. He'd said Tessa couldn't change her mother. The only thing Tessa could control was what kind of daughter she was and hope that, by doing so, it changed their relationship.

Maybe he was right.

On a whim, Tessa crossed the room and leaned over to wrap her mother in a tight hug. "Thanks for everything, Mom. When you have time, I'd love to pick your brain about ways to manage the power of the scythe. You know, responsibly."

Cheryl stiffened for half a second and then relaxed with a small puff of air. She patted Tessa's arm and smiled. "I'd like that, dear. Why don't you come over for dinner tomorrow? I'll make roast chicken."

Tessa left the office smiling. Though she almost couldn't stand not knowing what secret Mr. Blade had bestowed upon Cheryl, it felt like she'd made some headway in their relationship. Maybe they could build on that. Get closer. Be better.

And, of course, her mother was right. There, plainly visible on her desk, was an envelope containing the black card. Tessa could've sworn it hadn't been lying there when she'd got in that morning.

She sighed. She wouldn't push Cheryl. Instead, she'd do her best to be open and loving from her end. Maybe that would change the way they danced together.

In the parking lot, Tessa stopped to look up at the sky. She smiled and sent a silent thank you to Mr. Hanson. Wherever he was.

***

By the time she got back to Mist River Manor, Tessa's thoughts had shifted from Cheryl to Silas. She'd only seen him once since they got home the day before, and that was quick, as Silas had been heading to Mrs. Cross' apartment to fix a drippy faucet. And Tessa had been heading home to spend some quality time with Pepper.

Abi hadn't been able to get away from the tortie fast enough. Both Abi and Pepper had been disgruntled with Tessa, and she had some making up to do.

Abi was easy—she loved her gifts of a shirt, some fancy chocolate, and a huge bottle of moderately priced white wine. But the cat was harder. Pepper held a tougher grudge. Tessa was bound to be stuck holding the cat on her lap for many evenings to come—and probably springing for a few cans of fancy cat food—before Pepper thawed and forgave her.

And it had been fine with Tessa that there hadn't been an opportunity to talk much with Silas since they'd returned. She hadn't felt ready to face him and deal with all the unanswered questions between them.

But she knew it wasn't possible to avoid it forever. They saw each other daily. They couldn't go on like nothing had happened in Miami. Like they hadn't gotten closer.

Like Silas hadn't kissed her.

That kiss! Just the thought of it made the hairs on the back of her neck stand on end.

Tessa couldn't help worrying. Silas was smart and observant. He already knew something was off—Tessa thought he'd caught on to it from virtually her first day as a reaper. She couldn't see how there was any way of keeping him in the dark about her job for very long if they were actually dating.

But did that matter? Even if they decided not to be a couple, they were friends. Silas took an interest in Tessa and what went on her life, and that wasn't likely to change, even if they didn't dive into a romantic relationship.

As she parked Linda outside Mist River Manor and then sat staring at the building, Tessa thought about it some more. She remembered what Gloria had said—that it would be okay for Tessa to let Silas in on her secret at some point. Would that work? Could they have a relationship after Silas knew Tessa was a reaper?

Miami had proven that Tessa's job could be a dangerous one. Thankfully, Silas hadn't been put in danger down there, but what if something similar happened again? Them dating would mean he was around her more. And if he knew the secret, would that put him in danger somehow?

She didn't know. But as she watched Silas come out the front door of the apartment building and look around, stretching his back, Tessa did know one thing.

She wanted to be with him.

Tessa jumped out of the car and headed toward her handsome landlord, trying to screw up the courage to ask him out. His eyes tracked her across the lot. When she got to within a few feet, he said, "Before I lose my nerve, I have something to ask you."

She swallowed hard, wondering what he was going to say.

He stepped closer, grabbing her hands in his, and looked her in the eye. "I want you to know that I have feelings for you. I want to explore that—explore having a relationship."

Tessa let out a breath. She felt relief that she wouldn't have to ask him. Hot on the heels of the relief was more worry. Something in Silas' expression wasn't right. "I . . . I'd like that," she said softly, hoping that would release whatever tension he had.

But it didn't. Instead he squeezed her hands again and nodded. "Good. That's good. There's just one caveat."

Her chest squeezed in anticipation. Somehow, she knew what he was going to say.

He swallowed and then gave her a look that was almost pleading. His voice was soft and gentle. "If we're going to date, you're going to have to put up with me being busy with my job a lot. I get emergency calls sometimes when something needs to be fixed. If that happens, I might have to leave a nice dinner or duck out in the middle of a movie."

Tessa felt her shoulders relax. "Oh. That's okay. I understand. I can definitely work around that." She felt relieved that he hadn't said anything about having the feeling that she was keeping something from him.

"Good." He squeezed her hands again. "Good. I'm glad to hear that. But, also, I have to know our relationship is being built on honesty. So, if we're going to do this—if we're going to date—I don't want there to be anything between us, causing either of us to doubt the other one."

She nodded. "Neither do I."

"I'm glad you agree. Because if I'm going to get close to you—if you and I are going to give this a real shot," he pulled in a deep breath and then said, in a rush of words, "you're going to need to be honest about what you do. Tell me about your job—about the souls you reap."

Also By Christine Zane Thomas

Witching Hour starring 40 year old witch Constance Campbell

Book 1: Midlife Curses[1]

Book 2: Never Been Hexed[2]

Book 3: Must Love Charms[3]

Book 4: You've Got Spells[4]

Tessa Randolph Cozy Mysteries written with Paula Lester

Grim and Bear It[5]

The Scythe's Secrets[6]

Reap What She Sows[7]

Foodie File Mysteries starring Allie Treadwell

The Salty Taste of Murder[8]

A Choice Cocktail of Death[9]

A Juicy Morsel of Jealousy[10]

The Bitter Bite of Betrayal[11]

---

1. https://alsoby.me/r/amazon/B085GJLYCF?fc=us&ds=1

2. https://alsoby.me/r/amazon/B085J3DF8S?fc=us&ds=1

3. https://alsoby.me/r/amazon/B086R3HVRQ?fc=us&ds=1

4. https://alsoby.me/r/amazon/B086R8HMKK?fc=us&ds=1

5. https://alsoby.me/r/amazon/B085X2Q4LV?fc=us&ds=1

6. https://alsoby.me/r/amazon/B085X3L55M?fc=us&ds=1

7. https://alsoby.me/r/amazon/B085X2R3XL?fc=us&ds=1

8. https://alsoby.me/r/amazon/B07HGCRRSX?fc=us&ds=1

9. https://alsoby.me/r/amazon/B07J2VN5RY?fc=us&ds=1

10. https://alsoby.me/r/amazon/B07JN828F8?fc=us&ds=1

11. https://alsoby.me/r/amazon/B07N6MYF6Z?fc=us&ds=1

Comics and Coffee Case Files starring Kirby Jackson and Gambit
Book 1: Marvels, Mochas, and Murder[12]
Book 2: Lattes and Lies[13]
Book 3: Cold Brew Catastrophe[14]
Book 4: Decaf Deceit[15]

---

12.   https://alsoby.me/r/amazon/B07J2TFBCB?fc=us&ds=1

13.   https://alsoby.me/r/amazon/B07MRCJ56R?fc=us&ds=1

14.   https://alsoby.me/r/amazon/B07NKTHCDG?fc=us&ds=1

15.   https://alsoby.me/r/amazon/B07SYC5MV5?fc=us&ds=1

About Christine Zane Thomas

Christine Zane Thomas is the pen name of a husband and wife team. A shared love of mystery and sleuths spurred the creation of their own mysterious writer alter-ego.

While not writing, they can be found in northwest Florida with their two children, their dachshund Queenie, and schnauzer Tinker Bell. When not at home, their love of food takes them all around the South. Sometimes they sprinkle in a trip to Disney World. Food and Wine is their favorite season.

About Paula Lester

Sign up for Paula's newsletter to receive information on book releases, other fun information, book recommendations, promos, and more: https://sendfox.com/lp/10q2rm
You can see all of Paula's books at: www.paulalester.com

***

Works by Paula Lester:

***

**Beachside Books Magical Cozy Mysteries
(Co-Authored with Lisa B. Thomas)**
Pasta, Pirates and Poison
Apples, Actors and Axes
Grits, Gamblers and Grudges
Candy, Carpenters and Candlesticks
Meatballs, Mistletoe and Murder
Honey, Hearts and Homicide

***

**Crystal Springs Cozy Witch Mysteries
(Co-Authored with M.E. Harmon)**
Dead Witch Talking (prequel novella)
A Witch Too Late
A Witch Too Hot
A Witch Too Bright
A Witch Too Dead

A Witch Too Frozen
A Witch Too Soon

***

Isles of Mer Cozy Witch Mysteries
(Co-Authored with M.E. Harmon)

Sandy Seances
Seaside Spells
Bewitched Breakers

***

Cruise Ship Cozy Mysteries
(Co-Authored with M.E. Harmon)

Cruising for a Bruising
Angling for a Strangling
Yearning for a Burning

***

Sunnyside Retired Witches Community Mysteries

Ghostly Trails
A Bottle Full of Djinn
Loony Town
Mummy Issues
Clairvoyant Clues
Boss Blues
Engine Repairs
Wedding Whack
Turnabout Time

***

Sunnyside Magical Bakery Cozy Mysteries
Sugar Skulls and Suspects
Tea Tarts and Trespassers
Mint Macarons and Murderers

***

Superior Bay Witch Doctor Mysteries
Witch Doggone Killer?
The Affairs of Witches
Witch Way Out?

***

Unfamiliar Magic Mysteries
Infurior Magic

***

**Tessa Randolph Grim Reaper Cozy Mysteries
(Co-Authored with Christine Zane Thomas)**
Grim and Bear It
The Scythe's Secrets
Reap What She Sows